King of the Animals

YELLOW SHOE FICTION

Michael Griffith, Series Editor

King of the

Animals

stories

JOSH RUSSELL

Louisiana State University Press
Baton Rouge

Published by Louisiana State University Press
www.lsupress.org

This book is a work of fiction. Names, characters, organizations, places,
circumstances, and events are the product of the author's imagination or
are used fictitiously. Any resemblance to actual occurrences, institutions,
or individuals, living or dead, is coincidental.

Designer: Barbara Neely Bourgoyne
Typeface: Minion Pro

Cover image: *Fire.P,* by Motohide Takami, 2013. Oil and chalk on panel, 51.2 x 76.4
inches (130 x 194 cm) 2020, copyright © Motohide Takami/SEIZAN Gallery.

Library of Congress Cataloging-in-Publication Data
Names: Russell, Josh, author.
Title: King of the animals : stories / Josh Russell.
Description: Baton Rouge : Louisiana State University Press, [2021] | Series:
  Yellow shoe fiction
Identifiers: LCCN 2020027722 (print) | LCCN 2020027723 (ebook) | ISBN
  978-0-8071-7273-5 (paperback) | ISBN 978-0-8071-7504-0 (pdf) | ISBN
  978-0-8071-7505-7 (epub)
Classification: LCC PS3568.U76677 A6 2021 (print) | LCC PS3568.U76677
  (ebook) | DDC 813/.54—dc23
LC record available at https://lccn.loc.gov/2020027722
LC ebook record available at https://lccn.loc.gov/2020027723

For Kathryn & Lola, my favorite storytellers

Contents

King of the Animals

King of the Animals

I was soaping my armpits when Mom pulled me from the shower. The hallway was filled with smoke, and she dragged me naked down it, through the living room, out the front door, and onto the lawn. Across the street our neighbors were in their yards, their faces illuminated by flames and their phones.

I could feel the fire behind me, and I turned to see what they were recording just in time to watch our roof cave in with a sucking sound more wet than fiery. Without thinking, I said, "My fish."

Mom started walking, and I covered my crotch with my hands and followed, happy nobody was laughing at me but wondering why no one was offering to help. The Camry was parked down the street. We got in, and when I turned to ask her what was happening, why the Harmons and the Goldsteins had ignored us while our house burned, she wore what Dad calls the Swedish Mask: a fixed look of calm, disappointment, and resignation. I knew not to ask any questions.

She handed me a pair of running shorts. "There's a T-shirt and flip-flops on the backseat." These were the clothes my father had been wearing when we'd checked him into the hospital three days earlier for colon cancer surgery, and the Braves shirt still smelled like Tom's of Maine deodorant. When I pulled on the shorts and she started the car, I understood that we weren't coming back, that we were running away, and suddenly everything around me was heavy with significance. I'd learned to ride a bike on this street. I'd seen pictures of naked women for the first time in a magazine my jerk of a neighbor Owen kept in the shed behind his house. I'd broken my wrist falling out of the tree on the corner, near the stop sign where my mom always paused for two full seconds, longer than anyone else.

Another house was burning in our subdivision, and for a heartbeat I was relieved ours wasn't the only one. But in the next neighborhood an entire cul-de-sac was ablaze, and the relief vanished. We passed the fire station, and in the dark sat the trucks I'd loved as a little boy. There were no firemen to be seen.

On Memorial Drive I expected Circle K to be looted and Taco Bell to be no more than smoking ruins, but it was a quiet Tuesday night. The Y was open and the parking lot full. We got onto I-20, and here and there in the distance I saw fires lighting up the sky. When I tried to turn on the radio, Mom slapped my hand. We rode in silence.

My dad was to blame, I suspected. For months, on his blog, he'd mockingly diagrammed sentences harvested from tweets in order to prove the man who'd been elected was too stupid to be president. Even in the hospital, after his surgery, he'd kept it up, typing on his phone. Mom was sure he was going to get us all in trouble, but he'd scoffed at her fears, and more than once they'd ended up yelling at each other. When she went to ask the nurses about the transfusion he was receiving, he told me she was being paranoid. No one cared what he said about grammar, and the people who were mad about his criticizing the president were too moronic to know what he was making fun of anyway.

I thought maybe the plan was to go to my grandparents' in Tallahassee, and when Mom took I-85 downtown, I guessed we were stopping by the hospital to pick up Dad. But we didn't get even that far. We ended up at IKEA.

My mother and her parents left Sweden for Florida when she was fourteen, my age, but she couldn't forget how happy she'd been in Stockholm. IKEA always seemed to me a flimsy replacement— particleboard and umlauted perhaps-gibberish—but it made sense that on the night someone burned down our house, she'd choose even a flat-packed version of her previous life.

My dad's clothes were huge on me, his flip-flops two sizes too small for my feet, and riding up the escalator I felt almost as foolish and pathetic as I had walking naked in front of my neighbors.

We went to the cafeteria, and Mom paid for our meatballs with a twenty from a rubberbanded roll of cash she pulled out of her purse. "I knew something terrible might happen," she said, when she saw me staring. I was both impressed and worried.

Atlanta's skyline was framed in the wall of windows we sat next to. Nothing seemed to be on fire in Midtown. The hospital wasn't burning. We ate slowly, didn't speak except to comment on how good the food was, lingered over chocolate cake and coffee. The roll of bills made me sure the trouble wasn't limited to a few dozen burning houses. Closing time was approaching, and I hoped now we'd get Dad and make a break for Florida.

Instead, we wandered through Living Room, Sofa-beds, Wall Units & Media Storage, Kitchen, Dining, Workspaces, Bedroom, *allusion*

Children's IKEA, IKEA Family, and ended up back at the restaurant, now closed. Instead of heading for the exit, Mom turned back into Living Room. I trailed her to the model 430-square-foot apartment. She put her purse on the kitchen counter, sat down on the couch, and patted the space beside her so I'd join her. Employees in yellow golf shirts walked past as if we were invisible, and when the lights far above went off with a clunk, my mother clicked on a lamp on a side table.

I thought about the fire, being naked in front of the neighbors, wearing my father's too-big shorts, how I'd been worried Dad was going to die of cancer and how happy I'd been when the doctor told us everything went well, how Mom had allowed me to drink two cups of coffee on a school night. Then from the darkness came a woman with a kid on either side of her, a boy and a girl around my age—twins maybe—wearing what looked like each other's clothes, girl in a soccer uniform, complete with cleats, boy in black leggings and ballet slippers. My mother spoke to their mother in Swedish, and the woman answered in what sounded like the language I recognized from holidays in Florida but didn't understand. The twins and I looked sheepishly at one another while they conversed. Our mothers came to some sort of agreement, and then their mom touched their shoulders and led them toward Sofa-beds, her phone's flashlight lighting the way.

"What the fuck is going on?" I demanded.

"A pogrom," Mom said calmly.

It freaked me out that she didn't scold me for saying *fuck*.

In a forced cheery voice she asked, "Do you want to sleep up in the loft bed or on the couch?"

"We're sleeping here?"

"We are." She rummaged in her enormous purse instead of meeting my eyes.

"What about Dad?"

"He knows we're here, and he said to tell you hi."

"Is this his fault?"

She sighed. "This is the fault of whoever lit the fire."

Out in the dark I could hear low voices but not make out words, maybe the twins and their mom over in Sofa-beds, maybe IKEA workers wondering aloud what the hell we were up to.

"You take the bed," I said. "Couch is fine."

She climbed up, and I turned off the light.

When she started to snore, I found her phone in her purse. Mine had been charging beside my bed while I showered.

I checked CNN, the *Washington Post,* the *New York Times.* There were fires reported in a dozen cities. On a subreddit they were joking about Get-Even Night. Rumor had it the sore-winner president had called on his goons to punish those who had opposed him during the election. So I was right—Dad was at least part of the reason our house got burned down. On CNN the losing candidate had claimed this was proof the president was nothing more than "the King of the Animals," an insult that so delighted her rival, our president, that he'd worn a rubber horse mask for the entire press conference he'd held to let the world know the loser's claims about the fires were just more proof that she, Washington elites, and the lamestream media were in cahoots to smear him because he'd made fools of them all.

On almost every news website there was a picture of me, naked, standing beside Mom in front of a fire shaped like the split-level that'd been our home. It didn't take long to find where the picture had come from. My neighbor Owen, the kid who

time stamp

charged me a dollar to look at the *Penthouse*s and *Playboy*s he'd stolen from his dad, had posted the snapshot on Instagram. His caption read *LOL fag.*

◆ ◆ ◆

In the IKEA cafeteria the next morning I sat with the twins, and we made a list of what we'd lost: board books we'd had since we were babies, pennies flattened into souvenirs at zoos and museums, Bibles we'd been given in Sunday school, a bin of beloved Barbies, cross-country ribbons, Little League and gymnastics and ballet and soccer trophies, our grandfathers' pocketknives, backpacks filled with homework and art projects, sharks' teeth, a Nintendo DS, LEGOs, a two-headed nickel, a betta fish named Milky Way, a guinea pig named Mister Mister.

Jay looked like he was going to cry when Sarah mentioned Mister Mister.

Our mothers were across the restaurant, talking to three women with luggage-sized purses. Their kids were younger than us, all five of them little enough to be held in laps.

The twins were dressed more normally then they had been the night before, Jay now in khakis and a button-down, Sarah in jeans and a black T-shirt.

"Where'd you get clean clothes?" I asked.

Sarah snorted. "I wish they were clean. Our washer broke, so there's a bunch of laundry in the minivan." She looked me up and down. "I've got some shorts you can have so you don't have to wear fat-dude swim trunks or whatever those are." She got up and walked over to the table where our mothers sat discussing an IKEA floor plan.

I wondered when we'd go get Dad, and then it occurred to me there were no men at the table with the moms. "Where are all the dads?" I asked Jay. "Where's your dad?"

"Is it fun being a homophobe, *Lucas?*" he answered.

"Homophobe?"

"Maybe I don't have a dad, *Lucas*. Maybe I have two moms, *Lucas*. Maybe you hate gay people, *Lucas.*"

I thought the right thing to say might be, "So where's your other mom?" but it wasn't.

"Nice picture, *Lucas,*" he hissed, then showed me his phone.

"Dude, they burned my house down too."

"Sorry, *Lucas.*"

"Why do you keep saying my name?"

Sarah was back. She handed me the jersey she'd been wearing the night before and, holding up a pair of basketball shorts, said, "How do you feel about blue?"

"Those are mine," her brother complained. "And where'd you get that?"

She patted the messenger bag he was pointing to. "This place has everything, yo." The price tag was still attached. "And I got Lucas some big-boy shoes." From the bag she pulled a pair of slippers and snapped the plastic string connecting left to right before handing them to me.

"Don't steal," Jay scolded. "Stealing is wrong."

Sarah sounded like she was talking to a five-year-old when she said to her brother, "You're embarrassing yourself. You need a timeout."

"Screw you," he said, and took his coffee cup to a table in a far corner. I watched the moms watch him sulking. Sarah's mother frowned at her, and Sarah grinned and waved.

She sat down beside me, leaned close, and whispered, "I've seen you naked."

I felt myself blush. When she opened the messenger bag, the tiny, wise face of a guinea pig peeked up at me.

◆　◆　◆

Sarah waited outside the men's room while I put on her brother's shorts and her soccer jersey. The armpits smelled like flowery deodorant, not Dad's herbs and dirt, and to avoid a hard-on, I had to stop sniffing her shirt and try not to think about her whispering she'd seen me naked.

IKEA seemed normal. People ambled through its departments, paused to sit on a couch or copy down the aisle and shelf number for a patio table, then rejoined the crowd. Sarah and I fell in, and though I wanted to impress her by walking against the parade, it calmed me a little to be part of something boring. In Dining she took my hand, and we walked along not looking at each other.

I peeked and wondered if she was as relaxed as she looked, which seemed impossible, since holding her hand was making me almost hysterical.

"Excuse me," a woman said, and I let go of Sarah and stepped out of the way.

"Excuse me," she said again. "You look familiar. Weren't you on TV?" The people around her slowed, and several turned. The woman was wearing sunglasses, and I couldn't see her eyes, but I could tell she was squinting, trying to place me.

"Commercials," I lied. "For apple juice." Where that had come from, I had no idea.

"He complains to his dad that they're out, then his mom walks into the kitchen with bags of groceries?" Sarah said. She was talking about an ad for cookies, but the woman was nodding and smiling.

"Then I drink a huge glass and wipe my mouth with the back of my hand." I wiped my mouth with the back of my hand to demonstrate. That was from an ad for chocolate milk.

The woman clapped. "I knew it! You're great! It's so great to meet someone from television during these worrying times, you know? Keep up the great work!"

"Thanks," I said weakly.

The shuffling crowd left us behind.

Sarah smirked at me. "You're famous."

I tried to sort the fear that I'd been recognized as the naked kid standing in front of the burning house from the excitement of lying and having Sarah back up my lie from the thrill of holding her hand from the smell of her shirt.

"Why don't you tell Jay you have his guinea pig?"

"Mister Mister isn't his—he's *ours*."

I waited for her to tell me more, but she didn't.

On the far side of Bedroom, across a space filled with dozens of mattresses, some bare, some made up with sheets from Bed Textiles, I saw a man lying on a king-sized bed, a plastic grocery bag beside him on the brightly colored comforter. The woman who'd almost recognized me shook her head as she walked past, and the man gave her the finger. It was Dad.

I nearly ran to him, Sarah hurrying along behind me. When we reached his bedside, I leaned over and hugged him. He groaned, and I let go. "Hey, kid. I figured you or Mom would find me at some point." He didn't make any attempt to sit up. When I'd seen him yesterday morning, they told us he'd have to stay in the hospital for at least three more days.

"They burned down the house." I was embarrassed by how my voice cracked.

"Who's this?"

"I'm Sarah," she said, and took my hand again. "Lucas's girlfriend."

His look of surprise probably mirrored mine.

"Kid, that picture of you and your mother is amazing. You could end up your generation's Napalm Girl."

"Napalm Girl?" Sarah asked.

"Phan Thị Kim Phúc," he told her. "The nine-year-old running along the road after the South Vietnamese bombed her village with napalm in 1972. Surely you know the Pulitzer Prize–winning photograph?"

I knew he was hurting, and I was glad to see him, but we were hiding in IKEA because he couldn't control himself online, and I couldn't stand another lecture about how terrible everyone and everything has always been. "This is your fault," I snapped. "They burned down the house because you're a pretentious dick."

"Language," he scolded, but he looked hurt.

I pulled Sarah away and into Closet Storage Systems.

"What's wrong with him?" she asked.

"He's a blowhard know-it-all."

She frowned. "I meant why does he look sick." The tone of her voice made clear she thought I was being mean.

"Colon cancer. They removed a tumor, and now he'll have to have chemo."

"Holy shit," she murmured.

"Language," I said, and she smiled.

We found Jay in Children's IKEA, sitting in a tiny chair at a tiny table. "There're a lot more people," he told us.

IKEA was busy, that was true, but I didn't understand why his voice was shaking.

"What's wrong?" his sister asked.

"Something terrible is happening. There're a bunch of women speaking Swedish. All the moms are freaking out, but they won't tell me why. Don't ditch me again, okay?"

I was still angry with my dad for talking about the photograph of me in front of Sarah, but I felt bad for leaving him lying there and for not fetching my mom. "Someone almost recognized me from that picture," I said, trying to change the subject, kind of.

My hand was still in Sarah's, and she squeezed it. "Good thing it's not your face people noticed."

The three of us cracked up. Jay banged on the kiddie table, and parents holding toddlers' hands to keep them away from bins of stuffed animals glared at us. For a moment we were just three annoying teenagers making too much noise in public—and then, over by the umbrellas and backpacks in IKEA Family, a fat guy in an American flag baseball cap started chanting the name of the president at two women wearing headscarves.

The women hurried away, abandoning their shopping cart, and the guy in the flag hat high-fived a half-dozen others wearing the same hat. They looked like the scowling dads and younger brothers I'd see in IKEA in late summer, dressed in camouflage jackets and boots, walking behind daughters and sisters filling carts in Dorm Room Essentials to prepare for their new citified college lives.

"Nice hats," Sarah muttered.

"What're you looking at?" a pimpled kid only a few years older than us yelled.

"Just counting the stars, Cap'n," Jay answered.

The kid looked confused for a moment, then his eyes narrowed.

Jay touched both index fingers to his temples and gave a weird two-handed salute.

"Let's go," I said, when the kid started to point us out to his buddies. "I want a cinnamon roll." I was sure they'd recognized me. I hoped Sarah would believe I was hungry, not scared.

From the escalator we could see an armored troop carrier parked outside and a handful of soldiers in body armor holding machine guns and watching customers come and go. One of them was wearing a rubber horse mask like the president's.

"Why's there a tank and army men?" Sarah asked.

"Us," Jay said. "You and me and Lucas and our moms and Lucas's dad and the Swedish women and their kids."

In the Bistro I paid for two cinnamon rolls and a cup of coffee with a twenty I'd taken from Mom's purse. There were tables by the wall of glass separating us from the soldiers, and we sat and watched them watch us eat. I tried to keep my paper cup near my face, hoping that would make it harder for people to recognize me.

I whispered, "They don't have any insignia on their uniforms."

Sarah squinted at them. "Is that bad?" She was whispering too.

"Jesus, you freaks, they can't hear you." Jay took a huge bite of hot dog and knocked on the glass. The two soldiers nearest glared and adjusted their guns.

"Yeah, I think that's bad." I nibbled a cinnamon roll. It was warm and sweet and reminded me I hadn't eaten anything since the night before—I'd been too upset at breakfast, listing everything that'd burned—and I had to make myself slow down by counting how many times I chewed each bite. The cinnamon was almost gritty, the icing sweet enough to make my teeth ache. I licked my fingers after the second roll was gone.

"Damn, dude," Sarah said, grinning. "Hungry much?"

Her phone clucked like a chicken.

"Mom?" Jay said.

Sarah checked. "Yup. She wants us to come back." She took my hand. "You too, Sticky."

• • •

The 430 on the outside wall of the model apartment where Mom and I had slept looked almost like an address, not the square footage into which several pages of the IKEA catalog had been stuffed. Next to the apartment was a huge model kitchen in which Sarah and Jay's mom was sitting on a barstool, frowning at her phone. We split up to join our parents.

My dad was on the couch watching people bicker on MSNBC, but he turned it off when he saw me. "Hey, kid," he said. My mother sat on the other end of the couch, reading, and when she put down her book, I checked the spine. The title was in Swedish— Mom could understand the whimsical props.

"What's up?" I asked, and they gave each other a worried look. "I mean, why did you tell me to come here?"

"Can't I worry?" Mom sounded like she was going to cry.

universal
commer
experience

"Calm down," Dad said.

"Shut up," she told him. "You shut the hell up." She stood and walked out of the model apartment and off into Sofa-beds.

We watched her go, and then Dad said, "Nice shoes," and pointed to the slippers Sarah had found.

"I like yours too," I told him, and nodded at the baby-blue socks he wore.

"No-slip," he said. When he lifted a foot to show me the dirty white rubber zigzags on the bottom, his face twisted in pain.

"Are you okay?" I asked.

He nodded, then shook his head. "I was supposed to have yellow socks because I'm a fall risk—the oxy they were giving me, plus I lost a lot of blood during surgery and had a transfusion—but they didn't have yellow ones in my size, so I got these blue ones, and one of the nurses rolled up a yellow one and put it over just the toes on my left foot. It drove me crazy. I could feel those toes sweating. Probably it was the oxy that made me think I could feel that, though."

"How'd you get here?"

"Everything's terrible, Lucas."

"Do you mean cancer, or—" I pointed to the TV's black screen.

"Both. Listen, those kids?"

"Sarah and Jay?"

He nodded. "And their mom—and maybe another mom and maybe a dad, I kind of lost track—are going to be in here with us."

My heart jumped at the idea of being with Sarah all the time, but then it fell. "How long are we staying here?"

He shrugged.

"*Why* are we staying here?"

"Turns out IKEA has a tax deal that makes this place like a Swedish embassy, so because of your mother, we've been granted asylum, sort of."

"Sort of?"

He put his hands on his stomach and doubled over. When he sat up again, he was smiling a tight, fake smile. He sounded out of breath when he asked, "What's this about a girlfriend?"

"I hope she's serious about that," I told him. I looked to see if Sarah was close enough to hear. She and Jay and their mom were looking at their mom's phone, talking to someone on FaceTime maybe. I watched her tuck her hair behind her ear. "I hope it's not just some kind of PTSD thing because they burned down her house."

lol

"Whatever it takes," he said.

I looked to see if he was serious or joking—his voice didn't give it away. His eyes were squeezed closed, and his teeth were bared.

"Are you okay?"

"Right after your mom texted me about the fire and where you were, those hospital assholes dumped me at a bus stop without money or pills. A homeless woman asked me for change. I started crying when I told her I didn't have any money, didn't know how I was going to get here, didn't know if I was going to die on that bench, and she told me to wait, try and be calm, and about five minutes later she came back with two other homeless women, and they had a piece of paper with the number of the bus I had to take to get here and money for the fare. The elected president of the fucking United States had my insurance canceled and had me thrown out of the hospital and burned

I watched fix political figure

common experience

down my house and almost killed my son and my wife because I mocked him for not knowing the difference between *t-h-e-i-r,* *t-h-e-r-e,* and *t-h-e-y*-apostrophe-*r-e,* but three homeless women gave me money and drew me a map."

I sat down beside him and held his hand. "Did they show the picture of me on MSNBC?"

"I'm sorry, kid."

"What for? I'm famous. And I have a girlfriend."

"Has she seen it?"

"She made a joke about not noticing my face."

He started giggling, then groaned in a high voice and doubled over again.

"Sorry I called you a pretentious dick," I told him.

"It's okay," he wheezed. "It's true."

Sarah was talking in the kitchen. I couldn't make out what she was saying, just the sound of her voice, which I strained to hear over the hum of IKEA—and when I realized I was paying more attention to the faint voice of a girl I'd known for less than a day than I was to my father, who was suffering right beside me, I felt selfish and cruel.

"It's going to be okay," I said, because I couldn't think of anything else to say.

"Probably not," he answered. "Go find your mom."

◆ ◆ ◆

She was on the other edge of IKEA, sitting at a desk in Workspaces, like part of the display.

"Dad told me to find you," I said, hoping this would prove both that I was a good kid and that he wasn't a total jerk.

She didn't look up from her phone when she asked, "Is something wrong?"

"Wrong?" It took all my self-control not to yell at her. What wasn't wrong? Everything was terrible. Instead, I shook my head. "Who're you texting?"

"Gram and Gramps." She rubbed her eyes. "They're okay. Nothing's happening in Tallahassee."

"Nothing ever does."

She sighed. "You sound like your father." She looked exhausted, and it was only then I considered more had been lost when the house burned than what was in my room. "Don't forget you're still a child."

"I'm not a child," I snapped, sounding like a child.

• • •

I sat between the twins on a loveseat within sight of the model apartment, watching unboxing videos on Sarah's phone. There was no mystery. The boxes weren't gift-wrapped. Most were labeled, and if they weren't—and usually even if they were—the YouTuber told us what was inside before she or he began to open the box. Sarah and Jay seemed to have seen all the videos before. I'd never understood why people liked these, but now it was starting to become clear: They were wonderfully dull.

While watching a pair of women's hands unpacking a box of erasers shaped like tiny busts of famous people—Einstein, Mozart, Frida Kahlo, Ben Franklin—Sarah rested her head on my shoulder. Instead of the jolt I'd felt when she first held my hand, I felt an amplified version of the calm that watching the videos brought.

Jay said, "I'm going to the bathroom," then poked Sarah's shoulder and reminded her, "Don't ditch me."

As soon as he was around a corner, Sarah asked, "Will you be an outlaw for my love?"

"Yes," I croaked, and she laughed.

"Mister Mister needs food."

I wasn't sure how this was going to lead to me being an outlaw or how it involved her love. "Salad from the restaurant?"

She shook her head. "We're going to Target."

"What about your brother?"

"I want to be alone with you."

To avoid Jay, we looped through Wall Units and Media Storage and took the shortcut to IKEA Family. The soldiers were still standing guard, but Sarah grabbed my hand, and we walked right past them. No one said a word, no one gave us a second look. Maybe the picture of me had been erased from their short-term memories, or maybe Sarah had been right and no one looked at your face if you were naked.

We shared her earbuds as we walked along. The song she played had in it the question she'd asked me about being an outlaw for her love, and knowing she'd been quoting someone else was disappointing—but she wanted to be alone with me. Cars stopped at red lights, and planes striped contrails across the clear blue sky. A woman wearing shimmering sweatpants and mirrored sunglasses waited for her squatting corgi to poop. Everything seemed so normal that I found myself wondering if there had been some mistake, if there might be a logical explanation for why my house had burned down: gas leak, lightning. We walked past Starbucks. Inside, men and women stood calmly in line, looking at their phones, waiting for coffee.

In Target we went up and down every aisle, drawing out our time alone together. Sarah said funny things about laundry detergent, toilet paper, ice cream makers. We found guinea pig food in pet supplies. I saw her smile wobble when we walked past a display of Barbies on the edge of the toy section, but then she joked about the romance novels across the aisle. We watched a few minutes of skateboarding on rows and rows of TVs. In sporting goods I picked up a tennis racket and served an invisible ball.

"Bitch, I know you," a voice said behind us. We both turned. Someone wearing a horse mask pointed at Sarah. "I should rape your homo ass right here."

I threw a punch but hit only the long nose of his mask, which spun on his head and left him blinded.

"Run," Sarah said, but I didn't want to run. Instead, I swung the tennis racket as hard as I could. It bounced off his head, so on the second swing I used two hands and turned the racket, chopping him. That blow sent him to his knees, and I kept hitting him until he was curled up on the floor, screaming inside the backwards mask.

"Stop," Sarah said, and I did. The racket was warped. My hands hurt. Sarah bent down and pulled the mask off. "Mason?" The kid's nose was bloodied, and he was crying.

"Damn," someone said, and when Sarah and I looked up, a Target employee was at the end of the aisle, holding his phone out, recording.

I grabbed the mask and put it on. Through the holes in the nose, I saw Sarah's puzzled look, then saw her understand what I was doing.

"That's what you get for talking shit about the King of the Animals," she said, and kicked Mason.

Wearing the mask, I led Sarah through the store. People laughed, some clapped, a bunch took pictures of me. The world outside, as seen through the mask's eyeholes, was hard to move through. I tripped over a curb and walked into the side of a trashcan. Sarah didn't say anything. I replayed the entire trip to Target, from her asking if I would be an outlaw for her love to our leaving without paying for Mister Mister's food, and my mind snagged on one detail.

"Why'd he call you a homo?" My voice was shrill and too loud inside the mask.

"That's what you're thinking about? You probably cracked Mason's skull, and that's what you're thinking about?"

"Your moms," I realized aloud.

"Bingo. Maybe my brother was right about your homophobia."

"He was not!" I whined.

Even though the mask made it difficult, I saw her roll her eyes. "Calm down, Horseface."

◆ ◆ ◆

Jay was waiting for us by the bistro. "I can't believe you left me here. I was sure you were dead—then I saw this." He held up his phone.

I took off the mask to see what he'd been watching, and on the screen I was beating a kid with a tennis racket.

"Hundred thousand views." He looked and corrected himself: "Two hundred thousand."

Sarah was thumbing through the news. "'Get-Even Night Naked Boy Gets Even.'"

"I guess they were looking at your face after all," Jay said.

"It was Mason," Sarah told her brother.

"From school?"

She nodded. "He said he should rape me."

Jay hung his head.

"It's never going to be okay again," I said, hating myself for sounding like my dad.

I expected to be in serious trouble when we got to the model apartment, but the adults were all staring at the TV. While we'd been at Target, men wearing T-shirts emblazoned with the losing candidate's logo and campaign slogan—a red-white-and-blue thumbs-up, *These States Are United!*—had attacked a sports bar in Los Angeles. They wore balaclavas and shouted "God is great!" and "Death to America!" while firing automatic weapons. Nearly two dozen people were dead.

universal exp.

"IKEA is throwing us out," Dad told us. "Whatever deal Sweden had has been rescinded. We're going to Florida."

"What about your job?" I asked.

"They burned down our house and canceled my insurance. I don't think I'm welcome at the community college anymore."

"Say your goodbyes," Sarah's mom said, not looking away from the news. She sounded like she was picking up the twins from a playdate.

Sarah handed Jay her bag and opened it to show him Mister Mister, and his eyes went wide. He was babbling baby talk to his guinea pig and didn't notice when we walked off.

In Sofa-beds I said, "Let's go away together."

Sarah looked terrified.

"You can't," I realized out loud, and she agreed, "I can't."

"You're thirteen."

"I'm thirteen."

"I'm fourteen."

"You're fourteen."

"Are you really my girlfriend?"

She nodded.

◆ ◆ ◆

When IKEA fell, there were no helicopters on the roof to take us to Swedish navy ships waiting on the Chattahoochee. Our cars were still in the lot, untouched. Moms put kids in car seats and gave them juice boxes. I watched Sarah and Jay get into a minivan. They were headed for Maine. Online there were rumors that the King of the Animals had had a heart attack, that the vice president was impersonating him under the horse mask, that a Russian spy was under the mask and the King was in Moscow or Budapest or Kiev, that reeducation camps were operating in Texas and Idaho, that Paris was in ruins, London was in ruins, Barcelona was in ruins, Boston was in ruins. Mom merged onto I-75, and we headed south.

Two Photographs by Walker Evans

There is a Walker Evans photograph of a man standing in a barbershop doorway, his face half-covered in lather, half-shaved. In the window the perplexed barber holds his razor over an empty chair. The harlequin man glares right into the lens. His hands rest on his hips. The man is my father, and this is the story.

Evans took a photograph of my seventeen-year-old sister, Lillian. In it she lies nude on a bed covered by a simple white sheet. Her hair is wild on the pillow, and her left foot casts a sharp shadow. Her legs are parted. She showed the picture to me the day she packed, though I was a thirteen-year-old boy and knew nothing. The sight of her naked was shocking and beautiful.

While she filled a musette bag with her things, she told me how the photograph came to be taken. She and Evans were lovers, and one morning when my father and I assumed she was shopping on Canal, Evans took a playful snapshot as she lay in his bed. They had just made love, and she pointed to the smile she wore in the picture as proof she was happy there with Walker. Evans left town shortly after the photo was taken, and she was supposed to catch a bus on the sly and meet him in Valdosta, Georgia.

The last days he was in New Orleans, Evans feared murder by my father's hand. Searching her bureau for forbidden Lucky Strikes, my father had happened upon the picture of his daughter basking in a bliss whose source no one could fail to recognize. The day after, mid-shave in a Royal Street barber's, he spotted Evans photographing a grocery. When he hurried to the door and yelled his name, Evans turned with his camera to his eye and saw my father through the lens. The composition was too good to waste—at the base of the barber's striped pole a black cat, in the window combs and scissors in jars of antiseptic, his lover's father scowling with his face half-masked by shave cream— so he snapped the shutter before hightailing it down Royal, cutting down Pirate's Alley and through Jackson Square.

To this day, the picture of my father is tacked to the wall in his front room. A Western Union boy brought it the day after Lillian left, two days after my father received half a shave. There was no note, only Evans's studio stamp on the back of the print.

So far as I know, I am one of only four people who ever saw the picture of Lillian—Evans, my father, and Lillian being the other three. Why show it to me? I asked, amazed she had. Love, she told me, is the most important thing in the world. Everyone will admit that, but I want to tell you something they won't: Love is the body. Believe the body, she said. That's why I'm showing it to you.

Report Concerning the Occurrences at B——

An investigation concerning the occurrences at the hamlet B——, in the eastern prefect of V——, has been conducted; the eleven residents of B—— have offered testimony, which has been entered into the official record; all evidence has been seized and cataloged.

Ana M—— (age 8)
He slept on a bed of sticks and the sticks were magic sticks.
Evidence: Two (2) sticks (birch, each approx. 1½ m).

Jakub K—— (age 59)
I refuse to speak unless my pension is restored. I was a trolley conductor in the city before the rails were torn up in the riots.
Evidence: N/A

Sigrid M—— (age 28)

The city is creeping toward us. We can see it coming. When I was a girl, the meadows went to the horizon, and now smokestacks line up on the sky's edge. He told us he came here because the noise of the city was unbearable. Ana is telling the truth. Long ago lightning split a tree. Its branches were scattered, and overnight each branch became a tall tree. He took sticks from those trees, and he slept on top of them. He made a horn of tree bark and listened to a crack in the creek bed. I asked him what he was hearing. He smiled and said, "Don't pretend you don't know." We all loved him. Eva loved him most. I am sorry he left.

Evidence: Cone-shaped construction mounted on iron base (construction: approx. 1½ m (height) x 2 m (length) x 1½ m (circumference); iron base: approx. 1 m (height) x 1½ m (width). See also testimony of Ana M——.

Cynthia P—— (age 27)

When we told him we had nothing left to hold dear after the looting, he made from paper bags and tape what looked to me to be the hollowed stump of a huge tree and from it drew our lost treasures. We stood below, wished for something lost, and he hauled it up on the block and tackle and handed it down to us. Simon got back his atlases, Bernard got back his mother's wedding ring, Sigrid got back the overcoat her grandfather had given her, Ana got back her box of stereoscope cards and their viewer, Eva got back the arcade token John gave her before he was conscripted and killed at ▮▮▮▮▮▮▮.

Evidence: Six (6) atlases; one (1) gold ring; one (1) brown woolen overcoat; thirty-nine (39) stereoscopic slides; one (1) stereoscope; one (1) novelty keepsake, incised EVA LOVE YOU ALWAYS JOHN.

Richard Z—— (age 38)

He was a faker. I'm embarrassed by the gullibility of my neighbors. From the moment he arrived, he was duping them with simple tricks: Ask a fellow why another fellow looks glum, then go and tell the glum fellow his mother's in heaven. As if he'd read the glum fellow's mind! The machines they claim he made to bring the rain and to return our stolen things were absurd. It was the wet season. It didn't take a fool on a unicycle wearing a dunce cap to bring on a storm. And here's something no one will mention to you: That day he pulled all those lost things up from that big paper bag was the day after he'd gone to the city. I think he asked what people had lost and then went and bought replacements—or stole them. Evidence: No "machines" as described herein (unicycle, dunce cap, etc.) have been recovered. See also testimony of Cynthia P——.

Simon M—— (age 31)

I am a schoolteacher so I am no fool, and I served in the army at ▮▮▮▮▮ so I am no greenhorn, so believe me when I tell you he was a genius. There had been no rain for months, and our gardens were dead, and only the deepest wells gave water. Eva asked him to do something to help us. He constructed a machine he claimed would bring a storm—

it had one wheel and what looked like the crude skeleton of a bird's wings. He rode away from us on his machine, and a splinter of lightning came down. The rain fell for three days, and our wells ran over.

Evidence: No "machines" as described herein (unicycle, dunce cap, etc.) have been recovered. Official meteorological records show no three-day rains occurring on dates on or near those offered by Simon M——.

Paul W—— (age 47)

I admit I was frightened of him. I know he was loved—I do not deny Eva her love for him—but his manner was bizarre, and I am a man who has lived in B—— all of my life except for my conscription and service in ████████, and so I was afraid of him and glad to see him leave. I don't know where he went. Listen, one day in the field he rode a tractor and led some things—I do not know what they were—along on strings. I know I am a simple man, and so this is not frightening to you when I say it, but he made that tractor from thin air, and I do not know what he was leading on those strings.

Evidence: No tractor or "things" as described herein have been recovered.

Bernard R—— (age 30)

He made the wind write in a book: Wires connected a pencil to a number of standards, and the wind moved the standards so as to make the pencil move. Eva told me to leave him alone, but I went and asked him what the wind had written. He licked his fingers and flipped back a few pages. I looked over his shoulder while he read. It was not our language or any language I could recognize, but it was beautiful. His voice was the voice of a soothsayer or a priest.

Evidence: One (1) bound folio (approx. 1½ m x ¾ m); Professor ████ has examined the writing and proposed that it is a combination of simple code and an antique northern dialect.

Sylvia T—— (age 17)

You ask me, he was ugly. Bernard tried to tell me about the wind writing in that book, but you ask me, he was scribbling in that stupid book and then just saying the wind was writing. You ask me, he just wanted to be fed for doing nothing, and those stupid people did feed him. Eva even fucked him. My parents are dead, and I wish I could get out of this stupid village of stupid idiots.

Evidence: See also testimony of Bernard R——.

interesting structure

Max O—— (age 25)

He took Eva from me, so at first I hated him. But how can you hate a man who can stitch up a wound like Eva's? Of course there was the rain and the way he gave us back what we'd lost—this is my great-grandfather's watch, real gold—but it was how he made Eva stop grieving that I see as his miracle. One day I followed him into the fields intending to threaten him. He was walking fast, but I kept up. He stopped and bent to observe a dandelion gone to seed. When he touched it, it began to grow until it stood above us, tall as a tree. He shimmied up its trunk and hollered into the puff-ball, sending the seeds into the air on their soft parachutes.

Connects to previous chapter [handwritten note]

When he came down, he shook my hand, and the dandelion shrank to its normal size. This is true. But more important is the fact that Eva no longer spends her days speaking to a photograph of a dead man.

Evidence: One (1) photograph of Corporal Jonathan ████ ; one (1) gold pocket watch.

Eva H—— (age 23)

████████████████████████████████████
████████████████████████████████████
███████████████████

Evidence: ████████████████████████████████
████████████████████████████████████
████████████████████████████████████
████████████████████████████████████
████████████████████████████████████
████████████████████████████████████
████████████████████████████████████
████████████████████████████████████
████████████████████████████████████
████████████████████████████████████
████████████████████████████████████
████████████████████████████████████
████████████████████████████████████
████████████████████████████████████
████████████████████████████████████
████████████████████████████████████
████████████████████████████████████
████████████████████████████████████
█████████████████████████

Some Freud

In her dreams I'm again unfaithful with the woman neither of us knows in waking life. At first I found it funny when she woke pissed off because of something I did in a dream. I'm no longer amused. As decades pass, I'm more and more sure my college girlfriend cheated on me, but I'm fiercely loyal, and I've never cheated on anyone. I dream of memos and mopping.

Saturday she wakes me with the news she's kicked my girlfriend's ass, beaten her so badly, in fact, the bitch may be dead. What do I think about *that?* I've been dreaming of folding laundry, and this sounds like a horrifying confession—then I wake enough to remember the only girlfriend I have is the smugly smiling one in bed next to me. I offer the hope she's been successful at dream murder so she can quit fussing at me. Maybe, I suggest, she can now dream about me folding laundry.

We spend the day bickering over waking versions of the kinds of things I dream about—a rug needs vacuuming, a toilet scrubbing—and we're still sniping at each other when we leave for the dinner party at a friend of a friend's. Neither of us wants to *violence?*

go, but we haven't the nerve to blow off people we barely know, so we drive in silence to a gentrified neighborhood of narrow townhouses. As a teenager, I came from the suburbs with my friends to the once-grand park here to skateboard in empty fountains and watch people buy drugs. The park's grand again, fountains plashing, junkies gone.

I ring the bell and hand over a bottle of wine on which my thumbprint's smeared in price tag glue. It's a nicer bottle than I'd buy if I knew these people better. Our host has the same name as my dream girlfriend, I've forgotten until she's taking my coat. Mean delight fills me as I say it often as I can while she leads us toward the back of the house. In the sunroom a half-dozen people, all younger than me, don't stop talking when we enter. My real-life girlfriend stares into the corner. I look, expecting a man, but there stands a harp tall as a man. Conversation quiets as she crosses the room, sits on the stool, tips the harp against her shoulder with what cannot be mistaken as anything but practiced ease, and begins to play.

So this is the source of her dreams: Never has she confessed during seventeen months of full-time intimacy that she's a harpist. She's good too. A secret is a betrayal. She's betrayed me by keeping this secret, and while she sleeps, she's attempted to transfer her guilt onto me. I'll explain this to her when she finishes the song, something slow I can't identify. I'll explain to her some Freud. Eyes closed, harp between her legs, she begins to play another, this one brisker, still nothing I can name. Somehow I know she'll play yet another when she finishes and then another after that.

Pretend You'll Do It Again

+ imagery

If you're walking together along a dark street on your way to lovemaking you both know will be the last you'll ever share, pretend you'll do it again in the morning; use the promise of a sunlit encore to arouse each other on the lamplit sidewalk and to make less elegiac the last undressing of one another in darkness, the last coupling on the darkened bedstage (skin on skin like sunlight on sunlight); imagine daybreak and the promised one-more-time it'll bring: What languid luxury such promises allow.

"mournful"

Young Woman Standing before a Window

Will met Paula at a poetry reading. She was there with Emily, a girl Will knew from his Women's Studies class. When Emily introduced Paula to Will, she mentioned he was in the seminar, and Paula looked him up and down with a bemused smirk that tweaked her pink lips into a cute curl.

"Paula's home from Vassar to put her cat to sleep," Emily explained as they sat down. "We went to high school together."

Someone began to introduce the poet, and while he half-listened to the list of awards and fellowships the woman had won, Will wondered why Paula had come all the way from New York—where he was pretty sure Vassar was—to Atlanta to put a cat to sleep and why she was out at a poetry reading when home to do such a thing.

The poems were all about orgasms, which made Will both uncomfortable—he was in a crowded room in the English Department—and horny—he was twenty-one years old and hadn't

[handwritten margin note: connects to prev. chapter]

had sex in seven months. He tried to think about putting cats to sleep. In the middle of one poem—*You never know when your passionate, moaning lover is having a lyrical orgasm*—Will tipped his head to scratch an itch below his ear and inadvertently caught Paula's eye, and as the poet continued *the epic orgasm, a long-winded orgasm in which one lover plays the hero or conqueror and relishes his victory,* Paula winked.

In a singsong voice the poet went on and on and on about orgasms while Paula pressed the side of her knee against the side of his. *Dead cat,* he thought as the poet tried to fill his head with other thoughts, *dead cat dead cat dead cat.*

Thirty minutes later the reading was over, and Paula was inviting him to come with them for a drink—they were meeting Emily's boyfriend in Little Five Points—and then they were at the bar, and there was a pitcher, and when it was empty, Emily and her boyfriend left because he had to get up early, and then Will and Paula split another pitcher and talked about Judith Butler's *Gender Trouble,* which Will was reading for the seminar and Paula had read the previous semester, and then Paula said, "I can't drive, can you?"

Will admitted he couldn't, then told her they were two blocks away from the house where he lived. "I can sleep on the floor, and you can have the bed," he offered.

He truly expected he'd spend the night on the rug and in the morning maybe they'd get breakfast, not that he'd come back from brushing his teeth to find her sitting on the edge of his bed wearing only panties and reading the book of poems he'd bought and had the poet sign. "I like these," Paula said very seriously, not looking up.

At the reading Will thought the poems were silly, but now

he wondered if he'd made that judgment as a way to ignore their effect on him—he'd had to silently chant *dead cat,* after all—and on Paula, who now sat nearly naked on the edge of his bed. He tried not to stare at her breasts, which were small and pink-tipped, or her underwear, which was yellow with green elastic and had what looked like a green crest of some sort silkscreened on the crotch, and he wondered if she'd put on her clothes if he told her what he was thinking.

"Clearly, it helps that they're about fucking," she said, and grinned.

"Clearly," he agreed.

She set the book on his pillow and patted the bed beside her. For a few minutes they kissed sitting up, then he eased her back onto the sheets and they kissed some more. He hadn't even taken off his shoes, and that made him wonder if he was going too far when he touched her breasts and then rubbed his fingers against the fabric between her legs, and even as she kissed him deeply and moved her hips, he was still unsure what she wanted to do, how far she wanted to go—until she stopped kissing him and asked, "Why aren't you taking off your clothes?"

◆ ◆ ◆

Will woke to find her standing naked before his window, watching something in the backyard, and when she saw he was awake, she asked if he wanted to come with her to the vet. "Ever been to Peachtree City?"

"No," he said, sitting up. "That's the place with golf carts, right?"

[handwritten note: reoccurring image = sex]

She nodded. "Don't laugh, my cat's named Garfield. He's nineteen years old. I've had him since I was, like, two. This is going to suck, I warn you."

The way Paula stood nude in the sunlight—neither bashful nor seductive, just comfortable and alive—made him happy she'd asked him along, even if it would suck.

[handwritten note: time stamp allusion]

They found her car on Euclid and stopped at a Starbucks before getting on the highway. NPR negated the need for small talk, and though he assumed she was thinking sad thoughts about her childhood cat, Will began to worry that her speechless concentration on the road might mean she'd decided she'd made a mistake by inviting him. Between two exits a row of brand-new townhouses with vinyl siding stood in a field of red mud.

"I don't think I've ever met anyone my age named Paula," Will said to snap the silence—then felt stupid and blurted, "Will is short for Wilmer."

Paula laughed. "Family name?"

"Grandpa."

"Paula's my aunt's name. What time is it?"

Will checked his watch. "Nine thirty."

She nodded. "Okay, here's the deal. I have to get Garfield to the vet, and then I need to take a shower. My flight's at one thirty, which means I need to be there at twelve thirty, which means we need to leave at eleven thirty."

It was the first he'd heard of the flight. He'd imagined comforting her after Garfield was dead, driving back to Atlanta when she calmed down, drinking beers on his back porch, cooking her dinner, waking to find her standing naked in front of his window again.

◆ ◆ ◆

Peachtree City was a sprawling series of strip malls and subdi-visions linked by paved trails cut through stands of scrub pine, trails along which golf carts sped, most piloted, it seemed, by reckless teenaged boys in Auburn hats. Paula told him it would be quicker to take the cart, and she held the cat in her lap and directed Will. Garfield calmly watched the passing pines while Paula cooed to him. Will had never driven a golf cart before, and he was sure embarrassment waited for him around the next blind curve, but they made it to the vet without humiliation.

As he set the brake, Paula began to weep and Garfield to howl. Will led her inside and was ready to speak for her, then realized he didn't know her last name. Luckily, there was an ap-pointment, and they knew Garfield, and they acted like weeping women come to kill their cats were worth no more than a sad smile, and they led Paula and the cat into an examination room and left Will in the waiting area with a cage of kittens up for adoption and the TV playing *Tom and Jerry.*

He sat and watched mouse torture cat and wondered what was going to happen next. Seeing her standing calmly in the sun-light, his head cleared by sleep, he'd convinced himself there was more to it than beer and goofy poems about lyrical and epic or-gasms, and when she'd asked him to come to Peachtree City, his conviction had been strengthened, but now he wondered if he'd been fooling himself. Jerry hit Tom in the face with a hammer.

When she came out, Paula was carrying a cat collar on which hung a tag shaped like a four-leaf clover. "Okay, okay," she said, then took a long, stuttering breath and let it out. "Okay."

She drove the cart back to her house. They didn't speak, and Will could tell she was fighting tears. He wished she'd lose it, pull off into the trees, fall sobbing into his arms.

In the laundry room between the garage and the kitchen, she pulled her T-shirt over her head and unsnapped and shrugged off her bra. For a few quickened heartbeats when she pushed down her jeans and underpants, he was sure they were about to have sex, but she picked up her dirty clothes, dropped them into a basket beside the washer, said "I'll be quick," and walked out.

Heading north toward the airport, Paula told him her father was a Delta pilot and she was pissed at him for not being able to take Garfield to the vet—what kind of man has to fly his daughter home from college to put a cat to sleep? Then she abruptly changed the subject, and they laughed about the poet and her orgasm poems. It was clear to Will this joking was a way to talk about when they'd been together in bed, Will inside her, their arms around each other—the most significant thing they had in common, therefore the thing impossible to talk about—by talking about the brief list of everything else they'd shared: the poetry reading, Emily's boyfriend's ridiculous clamdiggers, the freakishly cheerful guy manning the Starbucks drive-through.

In the parking garage Paula used a fine-tip Sharpie to write her number on the back of his hand and his on the back of hers. She didn't kiss him. Will watched her hurry toward the terminal, not looking back even once, and wondered if he should be upset she'd been fending off heartbreak, nothing more, when she shared the night with him instead of with the old cat she had to put down the next morning, rather than happy that perhaps life could be so simple, her motives so pure.

Moscow

[handwritten marginalia: "rocurring o´ = love?"]

Before the war I was a pastry chef, a milliner, a streetcar conductor, the foreman of a vodka distillery. My name is Josef, is Karl, is Alexander, is Anastas. I am a Muscovite, I was born in Kiev, in Minsk, in Leningrad. The first lesson the agents from the People's Commissariat for Internal Affairs taught was to make every answer sound as if it is a lie. The first lesson was to make every lie ring true. The first lesson was the three-ball juggle. We were shown mimeographed diagrams, issued croquet balls, sent to the park to practice and to be sneered at by passersby for our decadence. The first lesson was from the musings of Comrade Lenin: *A lie told often enough becomes the truth.* The first lesson was: *Fascism is capitalism in decay.* The first lesson was: Nazis are landlords and noblemen. My love's name is Sunlight, Dirt, Wasp, Honeybee. I begged to be a member of the troupe. I was offered two choices: join and learn to juggle or bullet in the back of the skull. Dirt betrayed me. Sunlight groaned my name again and again when we coupled after curfew in a dark corner of the park—Vyacheslav, Nikoli. Shells screamed over-

40

[handwritten: Six]

head in the frozen, silent October air. Stars burned like bulbs screwed into the sky. The moon and the constellations were obscured by clouds. Before the war I was a juggler, a pastry chef, an electrician. The plan devised by the People's Commissariat for Internal Affairs is as follows: If the Germans break through the lines and overrun Moscow, we will offer to perform as part of their victory celebrations. The first lesson was: Germans like art, especially if it is not too serious. The plan is: If the Germans overrun the city, I will kill Honeybee's husband. The first lesson was: *One man with a gun can control one hundred without.* The first lesson was: *Every cook should be able to govern.* The plan is: I juggle three grenades, painted red, striped blue, and marked with yellow stars, and as the finale, I pull three pins and throw the grenades at the laughing landlords and noblemen. Before the war Wasp was true to me, she was inconstant as water, she wore a hat with a feather and ate decadent French pastries I brought her and washed them down with vodka while she rode the streetcar. The first lesson: *The most important thing when ill is never to lose heart.* The first lesson: In war the heart grows ill. The first lesson: *Sometimes—history needs a push.*

Negative Capability

After her wife dies (cancer, brain, sudden), she watches lectures her wife recorded for her students, videos she'd never seen while Pam was alive. They're about Romantic poetry—Coleridge, Shelley, et al.—and the university at which her wife had been an associate professor is still using them to teach undergraduates, which at first makes her furious, but the university's shamelessness means Pam's immortal online, so whenever she worries she's forgotten her wife's voice, she can watch a lecture about George Gordon Lord Byron and hear Pam's voice, or at least hear a version of it, a version a little more formal and careful than the voice her wife used for calls to say she was on her way home from campus and for questions regarding when the dog had last been out to pee and for arguments about spending ten dollars a day on oat milk lattes. She recognizes there's a danger she'll forget that voice, her wife's true voice, if she listens too often to Pam's associate professor voice, but she can't help herself. In one video Pam stutters while lecturing on De Quincey, and she's sure that inside the stammer she can hear her wife's true voice.

Same as 1st story

Then she wonders if the tumor caused the stutter, and for a few days she can't watch that video, but then she has to hear again her wife say *Duh-duh De Quincey.* The dog paces, disturbed, looks for Pam in the kitchen, the bathroom, so she plugs in earphones and listens to her wife's voice, close in her ears, close as it'd been when they lay side by side in the bed they bought with the money from the teaching award Pam won just six months before she died. After the De Quincey video she listens to her talk about Keats and feels guilty for not caring about De Quincey, about Romantic poetry, about so many of the things Pam cared about. She wants to write a paper about Negative Capability, to get it all wrong, to receive a pity C−. She wants to go to Pam's office at the university and watch her write helpful hints in the margins in a hand elegant and lovely as her true voice. She wants to listen to her wife explain her failures, tell her how to fix her mistakes.

An Airplane Control

recurring

Our previous king, tried and convicted in absentia but unable to believe his people would do such a thing to him, returns from tropical exile for some trivial reason—depending on who's telling, it's the third wedding of one of his daughters or the funeral of a friend's dog—and he's arrested on the jetway. His punishment is televised: The names of all the men, women, and children who died as a consequence of the wars he started are tattooed on his face, his chest, and the fronts of his thighs, kneecaps, and shins. Standing in front of the mirror each morning after one of his famous cold showers, he will read his shame.

None of us is old enough to remember the October evening they broadcast live him weeping as each letter of the thousands of names was needled into his skin (though of course we've seen the footage over and over in school). Just as their parents refused to believe men walked on the moon, ours refused and still refuse to believe the old king was truly punished. They've seen pictures of him on the internet, laughing and drinking Mexican beer on a black sand beach, his skin darkly tanned but unmarked. The new king reported that the old king had begged to be pardoned because he was no more than a puppet, and so, the new king claimed, after the last name was tattooed under his left eye, on the old king's back the tattooist drew a marionette's strings and "an airplane control," which, the new king explained, was called that because of its shape. There's no video of that phase of the punishment, but this part of the legend always rang truest to us because of the new king's much-mocked hobby: Punch and Judy shows.

Imagine how our hearts filled our throats when into the showers at the Y came a stooped old man who kept his back to us and on whose slack skin we saw tattooed what could only be an airplane control. We held him down, though he did not fight us, and there, on his sunken ribs, his bloated belly, the loose skin under his chin, were the names of our uncles, cousins, great-aunts. Names we knew from reading love letters our mothers kept hidden in shoeboxes at the backs of their closets and from laughing at what was scribbled on the endpapers of the high school annuals our fathers shelved next to the big art books. Names of generals we'd heard of from TV documentaries, names of selfless nurses we thought poets had made up, names of poets whose poems we had memorized for tests. The old king didn't say a word as we pinned him against the YMCA's tiles and pointed, read some names aloud. He acted like this happened to him every day of the week.

One Bed

Samantha's reading book-club Proust the morning her daughter, Fiona, calls from college to say she's bringing someone home for the weekend. Samantha asks, "Two beds or one?" and without hesitation Fiona answers, "One."

"You didn't ask *who?*"

"I was too shocked to demand the boy's name." Samantha tries to ignore Jim's glaring while hunting *Swann's Way* for her lost place. "I expected her to say two."

Samantha plays the CD of '80s songs nostalgia compelled her to buy at Starbucks when she saw "Love Will Tear Us Apart" alongside songs by the Cure and the Smiths. In high school she listened to Joy Division, wore Misfits T-shirts and raccoon eye makeup. Had Starbucks then existed outside of Seattle, she would've mocked brainwashed old women who paid four dollars for coffee and eleven for bullshit mix tapes. Samantha turns up Ian Curtis so she can't hear her teenaged self's taunts. In 1982, aged seventeen, she'd congratulated herself for recognizing the perfection of the tortured ellipsis between "Love, love will tear us apart" and "again," and as she listens to that pause and changes the sheets on the narrow bed Fiona's slept in since she was twelve, Samantha remembers changing the sheets on her own girlhood bed after an after-school assignation with her skater boyfriend Lance. Frantically horny, they'd agreed he'd pull out since he didn't have a condom, but because they'd never done it without one before, Sam hadn't factored in the mess—or the pregnancy scare.

Fiona rings the doorbell instead of using her key or trying the unlocked knob. Samantha's fallen asleep on the couch while reading; late-afternoon sunlight slants into the room. Jim comes from the kitchen wiping his hands on a dish towel, and she gets to her feet and follows him, but when he mutters "One bed" under his breath, she steps past him and jerks open the front door.

Fiona stands beside a tall girl with a brown bob who's wearing Buddy Holly glasses that match Jim's—*perfectly* match them. "Mom, Dad, this is Olivia," Fiona says. Samantha feels silence stretching, stretching, and though she has no idea what she's going to say, she knows someone needs to say something, so she opens her mouth to speak, but before she can, Olivia smiles and says, "I like your specs, Mr. Casey."

His voice is pinched when he tells her, "Call me Jim."

Samantha watches Fiona look back and forth from Olivia to Jim, her mouth open, clearly dumbfounded that until this moment she's failed to make the connection between her girlfriend's horn-rims and the pair her father's worn since she was in junior high. Samantha feels bad for delighting in her husband's discomfort and her daughter's dismay, but delighting diminishes her own discomfort and dismay. To hide her smile and break the second silence that's started to accumulate, she kisses Fiona's cheek, then, on tiptoe, Olivia's.

Winter, Fifth Avenue

Stieglitz stands in a snowstorm for three hours, ears burning from the cold, feet numb, mustache frozen, waiting for the moment. Fifth Avenue is crossed with cart tracks. The borrowed camera he holds, a four-by-five-inch detective, is capable of only a single shot. Children in scarves hurry along, but they are too small. Two workmen shovel a sidewalk. A glazier's wagon passes, frosted glass rattling. The wind snatches a man's derby from his head. There have been arguments, a scuffle even, over the worth of the hand camera. Samuel Leone claims it is too coarse for art, too simple. He demands a tripod, a huge negative. This horizontally blown snow, this avenue with its wheel ruts and gas lamps, this city of burning coal and horses with smoking breath, Stieglitz knows, will prove Leone wrong. The window of a nearby café is curtained with condensation. Above the wind's howl there is a pop like a pistol shot. It is the whip of a man driving his team—the ice delivery, cargo made useless by February. When he prints the picture, Stieglitz will crop away more than half of the image. He steps into the team's path.

In the warm café his ears sting and his toes tingle as his boots thaw. Stieglitz has wrapped the camera inside his scarf, and he drinks chocolate, bending over it to warm his nose. His mustache melts, shedding drops of water into his mug. The café is empty except for Stieglitz and a man who wipes the tops of vacant tables with a rag. Stieglitz takes his eyes away from the chocolate and watches. Diffused light spills over the man. The rag has been cut from the cloth of a dress, and its pattern is alive in his hand.

Grown-Ups

A cop blowing a whistle directed traffic into and out of Piedmont, and when he waved her in, Kim thought she could almost recognize the tune. She wondered if she'd ever visit a hospital that wasn't several hospitals stuck together, each mismatched building an example of its decade's generic architecture. The parking deck was an ugly afterthought, and the bridge from it to the 77 Building jiggled. HR was in the 1984 Building. A tiny wall diagram showed there were also Buildings 105, 95, 35, and 2004. The numbers didn't appear to be intended to orient. There was no YOU ARE HERE dot. On the gleaming terrazzo were yellow, blue, orange, red, and green lines, but corresponding lines didn't appear on the map. She'd been nervous in the car, and now she felt sick.

Kim could see the sign for Endoscopy down the hall and found it on the faded plan. To get to the 1984 Building, she needed to follow the hall to its visible end, past Endoscopy, and keep following when it doglegged to the right. She checked her bag to make sure she had her résumé.

When she was but a few steps from it, the door to Endoscopy opened, and out came a man who in profile looked like her dead husband. It wasn't Tom—she knew it couldn't be—but when she said "Tom?" and he turned to her and answered "Yes?" she made a fist and hit him in the ear.

"Are you crazy?" he hissed, and held the left side of his head. "Are you *crazy?*"

His cheekbones were slightly stronger than Tom's.

"I thought you were someone else."

He stared at her like she was speaking a language he had to translate word by word. His eyes were not as close-set as Tom's, though the blue matched. "Someone else named Tom?" he finally asked.

"Yes," she said, and started to walk away, hoping he'd assume she was indeed crazy and leave her alone.

Instead, he followed her. "You owe me a favor."

She pretended not to hear.

"Hey," he said, and put his hand on her shoulder.

She spun around and said, "I'll punch you again." When he laughed, he looked and sounded so much like Tom that she stumbled. Tom caught her elbow and held it. She didn't tell him not to touch her.

"Listen," he said, "I need someone to say they'll drive me home after I have my colonoscopy or they won't let me have it, and because I don't have insurance, I had to pay in advance, and I doubt there's a refund policy for a colonoscopy. And I'm missing a day's work. I knew I wasn't allowed to drive, but I thought I could catch the bus. Now they're telling me someone has to sit in the waiting room the entire time I have the colonoscopy."

"You want me to drive you home?"

He let go of her elbow. "Just tell them you will so I can have the colonoscopy."

A nurse in purple scrubs walked past, and Kim almost told her, "This man is bothering me," but she knew he was upset by the way he kept repeating the word *colonoscopy*, and she felt sorry for him. He looked hungover and had dark circles under his eyes.

"You really do look like someone I know named Tom."

"So you'll do it?"

She didn't want to. "Sure," she said.

Kim followed Tom into the Endoscopy waiting room, which was loud with TV and filled with people looking at their phones, and up to the desk, where he almost shouted at the receptionist that his ride had arrived, he was sorry he'd said before he didn't have one, he was just having trouble thinking clearly since he'd been fasting, you know, for the colonoscopy, and what he'd meant to say was that his ride wasn't *with* him when he first came in but that she was *on her way,* and look, here she was!

He was a clumsy liar in baggy sweatpants and a T-shirt with a picture of a squirrel on it. Kim was wearing her interview suit and grown-up makeup. She knew her fibs would work where his were failing.

"I'm his wife," she said. Tom flinched. "We're fighting."

The receptionist smirked and nodded knowingly at Kim.

Tom was called back immediately.

The TV was tuned to the talk show Kim's mother-in-law watched every morning, the volume so high it was as if the nitwit hosts were screaming at the celebrity chef who was making them an omelet. She closed her eyes, wondering how long she should wait before she pretended to go to the bathroom and snuck away.

Behind her eyelids she tried to keep separate the faces of the Tom she'd hit in the hallway and the Tom she'd often wanted to hit before he died.

The day Kim told Tom she was pregnant, he acted happy, which surprised her. They'd been married for a couple years then, and things hadn't been easy. She'd expected the news to cause trouble. They called in sick—both worked in the office of Tom's dad's pest control business—and spent the morning in bed having sex to celebrate what sex had led to, then went out for lunch, at which point Tom started drinking, and his mood changed. Four beers in, he loudly wondered how she could be so stupid, stupid enough to forget to take a pill, stupid enough to think he wanted a kid, stupid enough not to know he thought about leaving her fat ass every day. Kim saw the people at the next table trying to act as if they couldn't hear him. Tom saw them too.

"Hey," he said to the guy sitting to his right, "don't I know you? You look really familiar. Don't I know you? Are you on TV?"

It was a brilliant trick: Kim saw everyone's attention turn to the guy Tom was asking.

Then Tom looked to the left and said to a different man, "Hey, don't I know you? You look really familiar. Don't I know you? Are you on TV?"

Now everyone was looking at Tom. He pulled out his wallet and dropped bills onto his plate of half-eaten spaghetti.

He got up, and Kim followed.

In the car, she thought about abortion. She thought about

the cruelest ways to tell him she, too, considered leaving him every day but couldn't come up with a version that didn't sound like a weak echo of his meanness. She imagined him laughing at whatever she told him.

"Fuck, I'm sorry," he said. "I'm just kind of freaked out, you know?"

She knew this pattern and fought against giving in.

"Hey," he said, "don't I know you? You look really familiar. Don't I know you? Are you on TV?"

She heard herself laughing before she realized she was.

In the waiting room the commercials were even louder than the show. Kim asked the receptionist if it was okay to get coffee and was told that it was but to come back soon because she would need to be there when her husband woke from the anesthesia.

She was unlocking the Camry when she remembered why she was at the hospital. Thinking about Tom and having the receptionist refer to the guy who looked like Tom as her husband had rattled her. She crossed the bridge to Building 77 once again, hurried past the door to Endoscopy, navigated the dogleg she'd seen on the map, and found the passage to Building 1984.

A frowning HR receptionist time-stamped her résumé and dropped it onto a stack. "You could've emailed it, you know," she said. "No reason to dress up and come here."

Kim couldn't tell the receptionist that she'd been out of work for five months, that desperation had driven her to pick up her suit from the cleaners and borrow her teenage daughter's mascara, that dressing up and leaving the house made her mother-in-law hassle her a little less about not being able to get a job.

"Thanks!" she chirped.

The nurse in purple scrubs was in the hall, leaning against the wall and looking at her phone, when Kim turned the corner. "Good," the nurse said, "you're back. He'll be waking up soon."

"Long morning?" Kim asked, trying to sound blasé.

"Butts and guts. Lots of fun."

She led Kim to recovery and pulled closed the curtain behind her. Sedated, Tom looked like Tom had looked in his coffin—Tom dead for a decade, Tom who if alive would be thirty-seven. For a few weeks after the funeral, Ella, then three, had asked where Daddy was, then stopped asking, easy as that.

Kim poked Tom to see how deeply he slept. When he didn't react, she lifted the blanket to make sure his ankle wasn't marked with Tom's frat's three Greek letters. Instead, there was a tattoo of Big Bird.

"You asshole," she said anyway, as if this unconscious stranger were a conduit through which her years of anger could reach Tom, and immediately she felt stupid—this wasn't Tom—but he stirred and turned his head away slightly, and this infuriated her.

"Why?" she said, but he interrupted with a noise that was half-snore and half-sneeze.

His eyelids fluttered.

"I hate you," she said, and was taken aback by how good it made her feel to say it, so she said it again—"I *hate* you, you asshole"—and then she slapped him.

He yelped, and his eyes popped open. He looked confused and frightened. "What're you doing here?"

"Is the patient awake?" the nurse in purple scrubs asked in a singsong from the other side of the curtain.

Kim wondered how much she'd heard. "He is," she said.

The nurse pulled open the curtain and patted Kim's shoulder. "The doctor will be with you soon," she told her, not Tom.

"What are you doing here?" he asked Kim again.

"Sir, your wife is taking care of you," the nurse said, and Kim knew she must have heard everything.

"She's not my wife."

The nurse rolled her eyes. "Sir, anesthesia can make you confused. Just calm down." To Kim, she said, "They all wake up like this." She checked his pulse. "Just try to pass some gas, sir. Need to make sure everything's working."

"Listen, she's not my wife."

Kim could hear in his voice that he was becoming more lucid.

She suspected something was wrong the moment the doctor appeared—narrowed eyes and pinched mouth—and she was certain there was trouble when he began to speak in the slow and serious voice used to deliver bad news.

"I expected hemorrhoids, but I found a tumor."

Tom looked from the doctor to Kim to the nurse and back to the doctor. "Tumor?" he said, his tone guilty, as if he'd been hiding it from them and had been found out.

"Can-cer," the doctor told him, sounding out each syllable. "But this isn't a death sentence."

Kim knew the doctor thought he had to push the information through the fuzz of fading anesthesia, but the way he was talking to Tom made her angry for him.

"What now?" she asked.

"She's not my wife," Tom said.

"Sir," the nurse snapped at him.

"It's okay," the doctor said. "You're going to feel disoriented and upset. It's normal." He handed Kim some paperwork. "You'll need to make an appointment with a surgeon and an oncologist," he told her. "Call his GP and have him make the referrals."

"I don't have a GP," Tom said. "I don't have insurance."

The nurse and the doctor exchanged a look.

"She's not my wife," he added, and they appeared relieved he'd changed the subject.

"I met her in the hallway and asked her to lie so you'd do the colonoscopy. I don't even know her name."

The nurse and doctor turned to Kim, and suddenly it occurred to her she could get in trouble.

"Stop being weird," she said to Tom. "Get dressed. We'll get breakfast."

"I don't want breakfast."

The doctor patted Kim's shoulder. Bickering spouses were easier to believe in than the story of a woman pretending to be a man's wife so he could get a colonoscopy.

◆ ◆ ◆

Tom told everyone Kim wasn't his wife—the nurse in blue scrubs who helped him get dressed, the young, plump male orderly (his nametag identified him as Stanley) who came with a wheelchair, the men and women in the waiting room, the security guard in the hallway—and Kim felt bad because Tom was clearly dismayed that no one believed him.

In the garage she considered driving away, stranding him at the exit where he'd be waiting with Stanley, cutting him free of the lie that had allowed him to learn the truth about what was inside him and cutting herself free from thinking about Tom. But she worried again that if she did, she'd get in trouble—maybe they'd figure out who she was because of the résumé she'd left—and the possibility of trouble she couldn't afford, combined with the idea of him sitting in the wheelchair insisting over and over that she wasn't his wife until it became clear to the orderly she wasn't coming, made her sad. And truth be told, it had felt good to say to him the things she'd wanted to say to Tom for years. It had felt good to slap him. She'd buy him breakfast and drive him home.

She followed the signs to patient pickup and helped the orderly gently force Tom into the car. Though he'd stopped complaining she wasn't his wife, he nonetheless halfheartedly struggled as Stanley pulled the seatbelt over him and clicked it, at which point he slumped, defeated.

"Do you like pancakes?" she asked, as she turned onto Peachtree.

He glared at her. "Do I like pancakes?"

"My name's Kim, by the way."

"I don't care what your name is."

She stopped for a red light and waited for him to open the door and get out, but he didn't.

"You're young for a colonoscopy, aren't you?"

"There was blood in my shit."

The traffic light turned green. Kim couldn't think of anything more to say than "So, pancakes?"

He didn't answer. Out of the corner of her eye, she had trouble finding features that made this Tom obviously not dead Tom. She told herself time had made it hard for her to remember Tom's eyebrow, ear, frown, and that the Tom of her memories was being replaced by the Tom sitting next to her.

"Red!" he barked, and she stomped the brake to avoid rear-ending a minivan.

"My bad," she said.

He coughed and didn't look at her.

◆ ◆ ◆

Kim took him to a place on Ponce with a fading and flaking mural of a giant coffee cup on the wall that faced the parking lot. She'd driven past it many times and thought it looked interesting, but she hated eating alone in restaurants, so she'd never stopped.

Tom followed her in and sat across from her. He had his eyes closed. She couldn't figure out if this was because he was still anesthetized or if he was playing an angry game of I-can't-see-you.

Dozens of pastel toasters and hand mixers from the '50s hung on the walls, but the waitress wore a Motörhead T-shirt. A silver hoop pierced her lip.

"Coffee?" she asked.

"Yes, please," Kim answered.

Tom slowly opened his eyes and stared at the waitress. "Hey," he said to her. "Beth, right?"

She grinned. "You're Blake's friend."

He nodded and smiled. "Coffee would be awesome."

Tom looked like Tom when he flirted the way Tom used to flirt, when he looked over Kim's shoulder to watch Beth walk to the coffeepot.

"Do you want to talk about cancer?" Kim asked.

"No thanks," Tom said.

Beth brought their coffee. Kim studied Tom while he gave his order—pancakes, eggs, bacon, grits, large orange juice, raisin toast, fruit cup. So intent was she that it took a moment to realize he'd stopped talking and now he and Beth were staring at her.

Kim looked down at the menu and read aloud the first words she saw: "Biscuits and gravy." She sipped her coffee so she wouldn't have to make eye contact.

When the waitress had crossed the room, Tom asked, "Is this how you spend your mornings? Kidnapping people from the hospital and taking them to breakfast?"

His voice was sharper than before. Either, Kim thought, the drugs were wearing off or he was feeling less freaked out about the tumor or both.

"I'm just trying to be nice."

"You sucker-punched me and called me an asshole and slapped me."

Kim flinched. He'd been more awake than she'd thought. "I—" she started.

"Need to wash my hands," he said, and pushed back his chair and got up.

She felt foolish. What did she think was going to happen when she half-abducted some random guy who looked like Tom ten years ago, some guy who'd just been told he had colon cancer and needed surgery he couldn't afford? She should have told the truth at the hospital. When he came back to the table, she'd offer to pay for an Uber if he didn't want a ride, maybe send him flowers if he was willing to give her his address.

The waitress was back. A busboy in an apron stood behind her. There were many plates.

"Tom told me to give you this." Beth showed Kim her middle finger. She tore the check from her pad and slapped it down beside Kim's fork. "Whenever you're ready, ma'am."

"He left?"

"I'm sorry, didn't you understand the message?" She flipped Kim off again.

It made Kim feel old that her first impulse was to demand to see a manager, not to match obscenities with the waitress like she would have back when Tom was alive. Instead of doing either of those things, she handed over her credit card.

The busboy was walking past holding an empty takeout box, and Kim snatched it, sure that if she asked for one, Beth would spit in it.

"Thanks!" she said brightly, before he could complain.

She piled the huge breakfast into the container and realized running up the bill was another middle finger. Tom had never intended to eat any of it.

When the waitress came back with the receipt, Kim drew a dark *X* across the tip line.

◆ ◆ ◆

Outside she sat in her car and checked her email, hoping for a message from one of the many places she'd left her résumé over the past week. Instead, there was a note from Ella's math teacher about sloppy homework and low quiz grades.

Beth came out with the busboy, and they passed a lighter and leaned against the mural and smoked. Kim watched, remembering the innumerable cigarettes she'd smoked when a waitress, in the breaks between wrapping silverware and making huge urns of iced tea, between flirting with line cooks and counting tips: her life before Tom, before sharing a house with a mother-in-law with dementia, before a teenage daughter getting a D+ in math, before worrying unemployment benefits were about to run out.

His paperwork was on the passenger seat. The text at the top noted that a likely tumor had been discovered, biopsied, and tattooed. Kim wondered what tattooing a tumor involved. Below the notes was a grid of sixteen pictures of Tom's colon, four rows of four. The first dozen were of similarly shiny and weirdly clean yellow-pink tunnels. In the middle of the bottom row was a snapshot unlike the others—a bloody nub next to grayish pimples. It looked like someone had rubbed out a cigarette in his large intestine.

Kim got out and walked over to the waitress and the busboy. "Hey, Beth, right? Tom's sick." She held up the report. "I need to take this to him. Can you tell me where I can find him?"

Beth again showed Kim her middle finger. "Listen, Mom, how many times do I have to deliver this message?"

"You'll get old too." She'd meant it as a threat, but it sounded more like an apology.

The waitress flicked her cigarette at Kim and walked away.

"He works at Coffee Kingdom, over in EAV," the busboy told her. "Total dick, FYI."

◆ ◆ ◆

Kim disliked East Atlanta Village, its trust fund bohemians and belligerent panhandlers. The last time she'd found herself there was for a street festival Ella begged to be taken to. Her mother-in-law had tagged along so that she could go to an antique shop where she remembered buying things in decades past. The festival annoyed Kim—needlework samplers of obscene rap lyrics, weird overpriced baked goods, local bands blaring sloppy covers of songs she'd never heard—and the antique store had become a braiding salon, which first baffled, then enraged Doris.

It rained the entire time they'd been at the festival, so Kim was surprised by blue skies when she parked in front of the coffee shop. Through the plate glass she could see Tom behind the counter, smiling. The guy working the espresso machine had a matching grin. They looked as if they'd just shared a great joke.

Most of the people in the line Kim joined were dressed like she was: on their way to interviews or very late for work or running adult errands at once halfhearted and desperate, like midday adultery, or leaving a résumé at a hospital in the hope of being hired to sort files. Everyone at a table had a laptop and Buddy Holly glasses and looked like they'd slept in the T-shirts and skinny jeans they wore.

When her turn came, Kim could almost see through his forehead the gears of Tom's brain grinding as he tried to remember her. He was, she recognized, very stoned.

"You left this in my car." She handed him the colonoscopy report.

The edges of his smile twitched. He looked at the pictures. "Oh shit," he said.

His worried face was so much like Tom's worried face that she couldn't offer more than "Yes, well," and then, remembering where she was, "small decaf?"

Tom filled a paper cup and slid it across the counter. "Shit," he said again, looking at the snapshot of his tumor.

"Are you okay?" Kim asked.

"Come on, let's go," the guy behind her in line whined. "Dude, large latte," he said to the other barista.

Kim stepped aside, and the guy glared at her, tiny angry eyes sunk in a pig's face. He flipped a folded bill at Tom, and it fluttered to the counter. Tom picked it up, smoothed it carefully, rang up the order, and slowly made change, all of it in coins. When he cocked his arm, Kim took two steps back, feeling what was coming. Tom side-armed the fistful of quarters and nickels and dimes at the impatient man's chest. Coins bounced off his tie and shirtfront and clattered on the floor. The other barista called out, "Large latte," as though nothing odd had happened. The guy glared at Tom for a few seconds, then moved down the counter, picked up his coffee, and walked out, leaving behind every cent.

"Jed's going to fire you when that tool complains," the other barista said. "I mean, the fuck?"

Tom picked up the doctor's report. Discombobulated by the racket the coins had made on the floor and the sudden silence following, Kim thought he was coming around the counter to give the paper back to her, and she held out her hand. He walked past and out onto the sidewalk, still wearing his apron. She followed.

"You got me fired," he told her.

She was confused. "You threw change at someone. And no one fired you."

"Why are you here?"

Kim tapped the report he held.

He looked down at it and said again, "Oh shit."

"None to be seen in those pictures," she said lamely.

He squinted his bloodshot eyes at her. "Weed on top of anesthesia is hitting me hard. I'm super-hungry."

"I've still got all that food you ordered."

"Don't be mean."

"I'm serious."

"For real?"

"For real." Kim unlocked the Camry and opened the passenger door. The smell of pancakes wafted out.

"Can I have your coffee?"

She handed it to him, and he got in. Kim made her way to the driver's side and joined him. He found the takeout box.

She started speaking because unlike her Tom, this Tom didn't talk with his mouth full of food, and she couldn't bear to sit in silence: in profile the resemblance was even stronger.

"The last time I was here in EAV was for some street festival. It rained, and Ella complained but wouldn't leave, and my mother-in-law couldn't stop talking about how black people were ruining everything."

Tom barely looked up from his food.

"The guy you look just like is—was—my husband."

"Divorced?" he asked, eyes on eggs and fruit cup.

"Dead. Ten years ago. Car crash." Kim was still amazed he'd been sober and the woman who'd T-boned the Honda drunk. She'd assumed the opposite when the police came to the door late that Tuesday night.

"I married him because I was poor."

"There are worse reasons." Tom dropped the fork into the empty box. "You were, like, what, thirteen when you got married?"

Kim snorted. A kid on a skateboard clacked past on the sidewalk while zipping up his jacket, casually ollied a fire hydrant, landed in the street in front of a moving bus, and headed down the centerline on Flat Shoals.

"Who's Ella?" Tom asked.

"My daughter—who's thirteen and better not be getting married anytime soon."

"Kids today," he said, and tipped her coffee cup to get the last drops.

The setting was different, but she recognized the conversation's rhythms. Had they been in a bar, there would have been a couple more drinks and an exchange of information intended to make things less anonymous before one of them suggested they leave. In a coffee shop, now would be the time to suggest the bar.

"We live with my mother-in-law," Kim said. "Doris has dementia. Some days she thinks Tom's still alive and will be home soon to yell at her about what a bitch she is to not let him go to Florida for spring break with his friends."

"It must be hard to be a single parent." She recognized a seducer's twitchy smile. "And the dementia stuff must be hard too."

Kim imagined his room in the house he shared with the friend whom Beth, the waitress, had mentioned. What was his name? Blake? The unmade futon, the bong atop the IKEA dresser, the ironic thrift store or yard sale painting, the box of rubbers under the bed. Selfish sex during which no one took care of anyone except themselves and no one apologized.

"She thinks he's still alive?" Tom said.

"Some days." She was growing impatient with how slowly he was getting to the moment where he put his hand on her knee, so she put her hand on his.

"Do you think she would believe I was him?"

She pulled her hand back. "What?"

"The only insurance I can afford has a five thousand–dollar deductible."

"You want me to let you pretend to be my dead husband so you can scam my demented mother-in-law out of five thousand dollars?"

"I have cancer, remember?"

"Get out," Kim said.

"I'm kidding, I'm kidding." He put his hand high on her thigh. "I know you want to fuck."

"Out."

"You old cunt," he muttered.

Cold blew in when Tom climbed out. He slammed the door and stood on the curb for a moment, his back to the car, then headed down the street.

When would it end? Kim wondered. Everybody demanding favors, wanting their messes cleaned up. And what did she get in return? A waitress's middle finger, some Tom lookalike calling her a cunt, Doris yelling it was Kim's fault Tom was dead on the days she was lucid enough to remember he was dead.

She took a long breath and turned the key, and the reliable Camry started. Above East Atlanta's low buildings the early spring sky was a flawless blue. Kim hoped Tom would be fired until she looked down at the picture of his tumor.

She pulled away from the curb, drove past him, pulled over, rolled down the window. When he was parallel with the car, she called, "Get in."

"Fuck you," he said, almost under his breath.

"You forgot this." She waved the report.

He tried to reach in and grab it, but Kim pulled it back.

"Get in if you want it."

He pursed his lips and obeyed.

"You okay?" she asked.

"Are we going to do it?"

Doris was home. After school Ella went to drama club. Kim didn't have to pick her up until five. It could work.

"Yes."

Tom smirked and nodded. "My place is only a few blocks away."

"No, not that," she said, but for a moment she wondered if it would be better to do *that*, then explained "The copay."

"Aw." He sounded like Ella when Kim told her she was grounded for the weekend for saying something mean to her grandmother or not doing her math homework.

"You need five thousand dollars," she said, still weighing the pros and cons of sleeping with him. He looked so much like Tom.

"You really think she'll believe I'm her dead son? She's that gone?"

His question made clear she'd missed her chance at an innocent assignation. They were on their way to con her mother-in-law unless Kim stopped and again made him get out. She kept driving. Doris had days when she had to be reminded of the words for *fork* and *dog,* days when she made perfect cakes without a recipe, and there was no way to predict which today would be. The only constant was her nastiness toward Kim. "It'll work," she told him.

"How'd we meet?" he asked, when she stopped at a red light.

"Jesus, how stoned are you? The hospital, remember?"

"I mean, how did you and dead Tom meet? What if she— Doris? Mom?—quizzes me? What's my birthday? Did I play Little League? Did I call her Mom?"

The light turned green, and Kim drove through the intersection.

"We told his parents we met in a class at Emory, but really we met in a shitty bar where we got into a fight over whose quarters were stacked first to claim a pool table—mine were. I never went to Emory. We told them we fell in love in Shakespeare seminar."

She'd never before told anyone these secrets. Kim saw Tom's lips moving, as if he was repeating her words to memorize them.

"You—*he* called her Momma."

"Momma," Tom repeated. "Momma. Momma."

She tried to remember how Doris had acted when she left the house earlier. All she could recall was her mother-in-law asking why Kim wasn't wearing pantyhose if she wanted to look nice. Did Kim not own pantyhose, Doris had wondered.

When a couple of blocks later Kim turned onto Memorial, Tom said, "You know what's funny?"

"No, what?"

He chuckled. "You told all those people at the hospital you were my wife, and I told them you weren't, and now I'm going to tell some old lady you are."

They rode in silence through a few stoplights.

"How long were we married before I died?" he asked, as they passed the basketball courts at East Lake Park.

"Five years."

"Was the car crash my fault?"

"No, which was a surprise. You were a drunk."

"Okay, cool."

Kim turned onto Candler.

"Do I have brothers or sisters?"

"Only child."

"Do you?"

"Do I what?"

"Have brothers or sisters? Where are your parents?"

"I'm a grown-up." She pulled into the driveway and turned off the ignition.

"This is it?"

The brick ranch looked shabby and small beside the huge new house some dentist had built next door the year before. Since Doris was too cheap to replace the worn-out roof, a dark patch of shingles showed where there had been a leak. "They used to be rich," Kim said. "Kind of." She looked at Doris's house and wished she'd just gone to his place, but it was too late. She'd lured him here, and now she was out of options.

Tom followed her to the front door and inside. The living room, she realized, looked like the living room of an old person, full of fake antique furniture and a huge collection of dusty bagpiper figurines. TV noise came from the kitchen. Nancy, Doris's elderly toy poodle, came to greet them, wagging her entire body.

"Should I know this dog?"

She nodded. "That's Nancy."

He picked Nancy up, and she licked his face.

"Stay here until I tell you to come in," Kim said, and walked through the dining room into the kitchen.

Doris was sitting at the little table in the breakfast nook, staring out the window, her hands wrapped around a coffee mug as Fox News muttered on the counter. She bopped her head slightly as if to the TV's beat. Her hair was a cloud of thin white curls, and Kim felt sorry for her rather than mad about her insults and parsimony.

This was stupid and cruel, Kim realized. She'd been an asshole to think otherwise. All she needed to do to make things right—or as close to right as she could manage at this point—was to turn on her heel, shoo Tom out the door and into the car before Doris saw him, and drive him back to EAV. She'd stop at the ATM and get what she could. Then he could buy weed and leave her alone. Doris looked away from a commercial and smiled at Kim.

"Momma?" Tom said from the doorway, and Kim and Doris turned to him. He was still holding Nancy. Over his shoulder, hanging on the wall, Kim noticed the high school graduation picture of Tom she'd seen so many times she'd forgotten it was there.

"Momma?" he said again. He looked nothing like the grinning kid in the mortarboard. "It's me, Tom. I'm home. I need five thousand dollars. Do you have five thousand dollars for me, Momma?"

Doris looked at Kim, puzzled.

"He's sick," Kim said weakly. "He needs money for the doctor."

Doris nodded, as if slowly understanding. "Wait here," she said.

At first Kim felt relieved—Doris was going to give him the money, and he would go away—and then disgusted with herself for taking advantage of the confused old woman who took Ella and her in when she lost her job and couldn't pay her rent.

"Does she have cash?" Tom asked once Doris was gone. "Check might be a problem, right?"

Kim walked past him into the dining room and stared at the picture of Tom.

"Oh, fuck, that's him?" Tom asked. He shook his head. "I don't look anything like that douchebag."

They were all douchebags, she realized, all of them, even the ones with cancer. "Give me the dog," Kim told him, and he handed over Nancy. "Now get out." She gave him a push, praying she could get him to leave before Doris came back.

"The fuck?" Tom asked.

Kim would tell her mother-in-law it had been a joke or that he'd threatened her and made her do it or that she didn't know what she was talking about—*Tom was here?*

Doris walked into the room holding a pair of scissors and a cordless phone. "I'm calling the police." Her voice was even and stern. "Get out of my house."

"It was her idea," Tom complained, and tipped his head toward Kim.

"That's not true," Doris said. She shook the scissors at him. "That's a lie."

Kim was stunned. It was the only time Doris had ever taken her side in an argument.

Doris held the phone to her ear but spoke to Tom. "She told you to get out, and I told you to get out, so get out."

He slammed the door when he left, and Nancy began barking excitedly. Kim put the poodle down, and the little dog hopped up onto the back of the couch and barked at the world outside the window.

When Doris wrapped her arms around her, pulling her into a tight hug, Kim could feel the phone and the scissors pressing against her back.

"That wasn't Tom," her mother-in-law whispered. "Tom's gone, but you're going to be okay."

Our Boys

[handwritten: Connection to Dons in prev. story]

POPPYCOCK

We make the mistake of letting our boys open the Amazon box, *[handwritten: title]* even though as of late we've grown to expect that their grandmother's gifts will be nonsensical at best. Inside there's a Barbie for each boy. One doll is black. We act like we don't find the gift weird, don't suspect an attempt to humiliate us and/or make our boys cry. We waive for once the no-toys-at-table rule. They are quiet and polite, and we joke they're behaving themselves because we have pretty dinner guests. Our older son pretends to feed his doll; our younger coos to his. Without being told to, they eat their broccoli and put their scraped plates in the dishwasher. The Barbies watch them bathe, lie beside them in bed and listen to a chapter of Harry Potter. Our boys' grandmother calls, and we hand the phone to our younger son so he can thank her. *I sent you those dollies because the word* poppycock *is Dutch for doll's excrement,* we hear her holler. *Okay, Grandma, thanks,* he says, passing the phone to his older brother, at whom she yells the same thing, then hangs up before he can respond.

They fall asleep happily hugging their Barbies. Tomorrow, we assure each other in the hallway, the novelty will wane.

CITIZENS OF THE WORLD

We take our boys to Paris so they will be cosmopolitans, eight- and ten-year-old citizens of the world. We tell them to keep their voices down, chew with their mouths closed, keep their elbows off the table and their napkins in their laps. We tell them how proud we are of them, little gentlemen, not miniature ugly Americans. *What's different?* we ask as we walk along Boulevard Saint-Germain. They shrug simultaneously and look longingly at a kiosk of tourist crap. *Pay attention to the world,* we tell them. We observe our boys when they eat pâté, pain aux raisins, what's advertised as "hot dog" and turns out to be two slim frankfurters end to end on a petite baguette topped with melted, cooled, and hardened Emmental. *This is different,* they tell us. *Yes, we agree, but what else?* We're hoping for evidence their views of the world have been recalibrated, not that they've noticed ambulances in Paris have sirens that sound like cartoon donkeys. *What else? Penises and breasts everywhere!* our older boy tries. *And testicles too!* his brother adds. They laugh at our shocked faces and explain, *Museums! At the museums!* We consider confessing we're Santa in order to shock them into seeing the world anew. In the Métro they beg for a vending machine candy bar called Kinder Bueno. *None of that is French,* we object. *Citizens of the world,* our younger boy reminds us, and so they get their German-Spanish bastard treat. On the train some asshole busker's strumming his guitar and singing Oasis hits. We worry our boys are the ugly Americans we worry we are. We buy them Orangina when they ask for Coke. They sulk, our younger son mutters *French Orangina is sweeter than American,* and his brother nods sullenly. *Sure, okay, but is there anything bigger that strikes you as different?* They look like we've told them a riddle, and it occurs to us we don't know the riddle's answer, so how can we who raised them expect our sweet boys to know the answer we don't? We're halfway across the bridge on which stupid tourists have hung so many padlocks it will soon collapse into the Seine when our older boy claps his hands and yells, *It's you! You're different!* The younger dances a spastic jig. Both of them grin like fools. They're delighted to have solved the riddle, but the solution leaves us depressed. We wanted *them* to be made different by Paris. A week away from work of course makes us different. Inside Sainte-Chapelle they bicker under a rose window, our same little boys, and we think about the trip home to Atlanta, worry about the short layover in Detroit, dread the email inboxes awaiting us. One more day of difference—French strawberries sweet as jam, Leffe for the price of High Life, bad news in a language we cannot understand—and then it's back to normal.

GOOD PEOPLE

We take our boys to church. It's been a while. We remember HELLO MY NAME IS badges stuck between their tiny shoulder blades when we picked them up from the childcare room the last time we came, our names on those stickers as if our boys were too young to have names of their own. Now they're old enough to sit through the service, younger studying the hymnal, older reading the Dickens novel he bought at a neighbor's yard sale. Christmas is coming, and we've chosen a service cen-

hml [handwritten]

tered on carols. Nevertheless, there is a sermon. We worry about our boys, worry without religion they'll end up like the boys who send via Snapchat and WhatsApp emojis of bombs and warnings to stay away from school if you want to be safe, worry with religion they'll end up like the boys we see brooding over laptops and red-letter New Testaments in jerkwater Starbucks when we drive down to Orlando to visit our boys' grandmother. Or maybe we've got it backwards, maybe those texted threats are because of religion and the boys with shaggy bowl cuts and Bibles are nonbelievers trying to pick up church girls. Antarctica is melting, and men and women with assault rifles are killing people in Paris and California. The internet's cluttered with hardcore porn and bomb-making tutorials. We hope our boys become good people, somehow. We pray for peace.

trauma of war + trauma [handwritten, right margin]

BLIZZARD

We're relieved to see our boys' matching backpacks sitting side by side in the kitchen the Friday afternoon the blizzard sends us home early from work. Neither answers when we call their names. We figure they're deafened by earbuds, distracted by homework. We go to our bedroom and change into sweatpants and weekend T-shirts. The walls are thin, the house is quiet as snow falls on and around it, and we hear moaning from our older boy's room. Never before have we heard either of our sons make these kinds of noises—and then we hear a woman. We tiptoe down the hall and find the younger boy's room empty. No one's in the family room, living room, dining room. Two backpacks in the kitchen, sounds of sex, brothers aged fifteen and seventeen, Wi-Fi, Christmas laptops: They're watching internet pornography—and then our younger son opens the back door and greats us loudly and happily, his shoulders and the brim of his Braves cap frosted with snow. When he drops his backpack, there're three in a row. He heads for the basement to hunt for the sled. Shortly thereafter our older boy comes into the kitchen, wild-eyed, followed by a pretty girl we know but not by name. Their clothes are carefully buttoned. We make hot chocolate and sit sipping it in the breakfast nook, and we study our older boy and his friend while we chat about the storm and watch his little brother climb the hill behind the house and then slide down. We cut our boy's fingernails until he was eleven. This girl's parents probably trimmed hers until she was that old. He'll walk her home soon, he says; he'll make sure she gets through the blizzard okay. She smiles but doesn't look at him. They're trying to keep between themselves a chaste distance, but the space grows smaller each time we look away to check the falling snow.

SNAPSHOTS

We dress our second son in his brother's hand-me-downs. As children, our boys' faces and haircuts are so alike that later we can't figure out in snapshots which one's which unless they both appear, so we halve the stack of photographs in which they're alone, make two albums, label the first with the firstborn's name, the second with the second's. Our boys don't notice. They bring home girlfriends, boyfriends, wives, offspring. Nobody figures it out. First the secret's delightful—we've tricked our clever kids!— then troubling. We thought we'd made our boys carefully, raised two individuals. We thought we were exhausted because we'd loved each with unique fervor. How can we now not recognize their differences? We study missing teeth, the Snoopy T-shirt's faded collar, the varying weight of Charlie the calico cat in their laps. When the phone rings in the middle of the night, we worry it's one of our boys, and if we answer and he greets us, we won't know to whom we're speaking.

Suburban Folktales

Turn the pages forward, and the man becomes a bird; turn
them back, and the bird becomes a man once more.
　　—Italo Calvino, "The Canary Prince"

THE DAUGHTER OF THE SUN

Married, the Sun's daughter became like all other women and
did no more strange things, but while in the carpool line, alone
inside the minivan, she remembers her wild youth. Teenaged,
the Sun's daughter took moody boys to the dark side of the
moon to smoke cigarettes and let them feel her up, hidden there
from her dad's bright sight. When their girlfriends cornered her
in the locker room after gym, she lifted her head off her shoulders and brushed her hair with her head cradled like a baby in
the crook of one elbow, and they ran screaming. Her worried
mother told her early and repeatedly the narrative of her con-
ception—sunbeam up Mom's skirt while she innocently climbed
a tree at a church picnic—but the Sun's daughter failed to hear
it as a morality tale, in part because at twelve, fourteen, sixteen,

she recognized lies: What nineteen-year-old *innocently* climbs a tree at a picnic? Who doesn't know what the Sun—or any man—will do when shown a pale thigh? Her husband's a redhead. The Sun's daughter's pale thigh had been too much for him to resist; the two of them made one luminous flesh the long night they met, winter solstice, hours and hours and hours away from the Sun. They married because of the baby but also because he hated the Sun and because the Sun hated him. The Sun's daughter happily settled down, kept her head while she grew big as the moon, gave birth on the longest day of the year, of course to a towhead—and here he is now, climbing into the car seat, smiling, holding a simple crayon drawing of his grandfather.

THE PALACE OF THE DOOMED QUEEN

She found herself in a room where a queen was chained and darting flames from her mouth, ears, and nose. Outside, a hurricane howled. The queen was handcuffed to the radiator. When she tried to ease away from the queen, the handcuffs jerked her arm back: The doomed queen across the room was her reflection in a clouded mirror. She remembered washing down a button of peyote with Big Shot pineapple pop. The plan had been to get a little loaded before evacuating, but the king was gone, and the handcuff bit her wrist.

Night passed, and in the morning she found herself in a room filling slowly with water. The sky outside the windows was the bleached color of a headache, and the creepy silence reminded her of the morning every fall when the heat broke and all the ACs in the neighborhood went quiet. The couch began to float. The doomed queen put her hand to her mouth and burned it off and was free of the cuffs. There were sharks and alligators and a pink dolphin swimming in the river the street had become. The doomed queen stood on her tiny porch in ankle-deep slop. The storm came and left and was alive maybe still. Maybe it and the king had gone off together.

She found herself wishing the king's corpse would float past, hands eaten by sharks and alligators. Instead, up bobbed a giant foam finger. The doomed queen slid it over her stump. Her flames burned blue as she thought of the king and tried to remember his reason for locking her to the radiator.

A johnboat parted the murky waters, and with her huge purple finger the doomed queen hailed the old man at the outboard. When he tied up to the porch rail, she revealed her stump, eager to shock someone with her misfortune. "Plunge it into the flood," he said calmly. "Get back what you lost." The water at her feet became clear, and in the mouth of a fish she saw a diadem set with precious gems. She stuck her mutilated arm into the water, and her hand grew back, but the fish darted away when she reached for the crown.

THE HANDMADE KING

"Papa," she replied, "if you would have me marry, give me one hundred and seventy-six pounds of flour and the same measure of sugar, for I want to create my betrothed with my own two hands." Her father worried she was a lesbian—thirty-three years old and no husband, no boyfriend, Obama sticker on her Civic, unshaved armpits at the public pool, Women's Studies PhD, highfalutin sarcasm. He worried she'd embarrass him in front of neighbors and coworkers. He nagged and nagged about marriage until one morning she joked about a handmade husband. That night she came home from work at the community college to the house she shared with him to find in the dining room neat pyramids of Domino granulated and Gold Medal bleached all-purpose: three hundred and fifty-two pounds of sugar and flour. Poker-faced, she said, "Going to be a fat dude." Her father nodded slowly, lips pursed. She shrugged and opined, "Bigger the cushion, better the pushin.'"

When not exhausted by a long day's labor, she could acknowledge her father sometimes meant well. After her mother died, he'd found himself with a daughter he'd been able to ignore wasn't a son until she needed a bra and began staying out past curfew with boys of whom he didn't approve. Often she wondered why he worried she was gay. Didn't he remember those boys? Maybe he did; maybe he figured they'd soured her on heterosexuality.

She couldn't sleep. On the kitchen counter she fashioned from sugar and flour a penis the size of her forearm, took a picture of her handiwork, sent the snapshot to her friend the folklorist from the women's college, then felt stupid for being so juvenile. *New boyfriend?* the folklorist texted back. Why *not* make a man? she thought. In the bowl in which her mother once mixed waffle batter, she stirred the stuff of a husband.

She made him the way she wanted, though she knew it was dangerous to desire something without a past. His bones she baked on cookie sheets. Around them she formed a golem of memories, pieces of men she'd loved and some she hadn't. Pepper for a nose. As a joke, three testicles: one a chestnut, one a walnut, one a hazelnut. She slapped him awake and led him to bed. Atop him, she banged the headboard against the wall. "Your father will hear," King Pepper worried. "That's the point," she told him.

King Pepper watched Fox News with her dad, got high with the stoner kid next door, stared blankly at the after-dinner movie the folklorist played. "I can't understand anything they're saying," he admitted. "It's French," the folklorist explained. He was void of anecdotes about high school, had no exes to friend on Facebook. His only scars she'd given him. Of course her friend the folklorist had sex with King Pepper.

There was a scene involving yelling, but neither she nor the folklorist gave it their all. Pepper stood in the kitchen and pretended to read the ingredients list on a bag of organic gingersnaps. He had a bruise on his neck her teeth had not left, a move in bed she had not taught him, and at least one inside joke she was outside of—therefore they lived happily ever after.

WOODEN MARIA

"He tethered Horseradish in a meadow, and nobody could steal him, for during his stay in the Devil's stables, the horse had learned to eat humans," one of Maria's fellow convent school alumnae claims. These quote-unquote princesses have had a few, and now they're one-upping each other with tales of kindnesses—to wrynecks, the Jordan River, hunchbacks, rake gates, dead men they covered with green boughs—and catalogs of good fortune gained from these acts: magic rhyming couplets, drowned ogresses, towheaded heirs, murderous carnivorous horses.

Wooden Maria's heard it all before. Any other Friday night she'd be laughing and bragging too—about the wooden dress her nursemaid constructed that let her walk on the sea, about the gown she demanded that was the color of said sea, all the fish embroidered in gold—but tonight she's wishing these bitches gowns of pitch and greatcoats of fire. Her stepmom's been texting her all day. Maria's dad's in the hospital, heart failing, lungs filling with water—which is maybe why she's thinking about walking across the sea and that gown with the fish.

She tries to tell a joke about the widow's recycling bin, how when she was walking her third grader to school she saw two dozen wine bottles, but her heart's not in it, and it goes over poorly, in part because she and her buddies have tonight downed a methuselah of red, in part because they fear becoming the hook-nosed former beauty who recycles her shame. All these dead men and their woebegone wives: the widow, soon her stepmother, in good time Maria and her peers. The youngest woman in the room checks her watch, and the party's over.

Maria wants to know: Where are the lost churchyards in which healing herbs grow, the grasses our grandfathers claimed revived their dead lovers? Sure, a cake with three hundred crowns baked inside, a goat that defecates ducats, a turnip big enough to hide a trapdoor that leads to an underground palace— but will our children rush to us when we're about to breathe our last?

THE SHIP WITH THREE DECKS
"But the old sailor had brought along the barrel containing the water of long life, in which he immersed the youth's body, only to see him jump right back out as sound as ever and so handsome that the king's daughter threw her arms around his neck." The man with cancer stopped reading aloud the article he'd found online and looked up at his colorectal surgeon.

"Kamat's water-of-long-life clinical trial," his surgeon said. "The results look promising"—the man's heart rose up—"but your HMO doesn't cover trials"—and then his heart fell.

Nevertheless, the man's HMO did cover the removal of a malignant tumor and ten inches of colon.

Not dying from stage III cancer was objectively wonderful, but the man envied the healed youth in the clinical trial. The youth's recovery time was instantaneous. Instead of shuffling along a hospital corridor as soon as he awoke from anesthesia so he wouldn't get blood clots, his surly twin sister holding his elbow so he wouldn't fall, the youth in the clinical trial gained for his ailments a princess's adoration. Instead of a chemotherapy appointment schedule, the youth inherited a kingdom.

"Nothing good comes from comparing yourself to people on the internet," the man's sister judged.

A coworker named Brandon visited him the day he came home. "Shit, man, after I heard about yours, I went to the doctor. Mine's stage IV, in my liver and my lungs. But at least we're not as fucked as Steve in HR. He has an inoperable brain tumor."

When first he'd been diagnosed, the man felt weirdly special. Nothing unique ever happened to him. But it turned out everyone had once had cancer or had a family history of cancer, or they, too, were in the process of losing innards and hair and breasts. It was as if every goat shat gold coins, every beggarwoman were a fairy, every cat an obscure royal suffering a curse. At first this depressed him—he wanted to be singular, not part of a team whose members pinned color-coded ribbons to their lapels and for whom healthy people ran 5Ks—but as he grew stronger, he began to understand it was better to be part of something so common it earned him but a few weeks of attention and pity. Better to be alive, to lie on the couch and listen to the rain on the patio umbrella while on the muted TV a baseball game in sunny Los Angeles gently unfolded like a piece of enchanted parchment.

SLEEPING BEAUTY AND HER CHILDREN

The young king's love was so intense that the sleeping maiden gave birth to twins, a boy and a girl, and you never saw two more beautiful children in your life. Childbirth's agonies broke the curse put upon Beauty in 1992. When the spindle's prick knocked out their then-teenaged daughter, Beauty's mother and father had built in their backyard a tiny castle without a door and inside it laid Beauty's warm, insensate body on her narrow childhood bed. During the decades she slept, the neighborhood changed. Her parents were the last royals on the block when they died, the old king a week after the old queen.

The young king was a flipper, and he found Beauty asleep in the weird stone outbuilding behind the brick rancher for which he'd paid nickels on the dollar. The neighborhood was changing again, coffeehouse and record store replacing wig shop and title loan place in storefronts where once upon a time there'd been mom-and-pop hardware and shoe repair. Republicans-with-gay-friends who paid top dollar for charter schools and original woodwork were replacing the Hondurans and Somalis who'd replaced mom and pop. Because the castle in the backyard had no door, the young king climbed a tree to reach its high window. Through it he saw Beauty and was so stunned he fell from the magnolia. His wrist felt broken, but he climbed up again. When he couldn't rouse the sleeping maiden, he undressed and joined her under a sheet embroidered in gold thread with a map of a kingdom that no longer existed. Nine months later, the babies roused Beauty.

Beauty awoke to screaming she didn't first recognize as her own, so long had it been since she'd used her voice. Pain sobered and exhausted her. She wanted to go back to sleep. A pair of hands in gardening gloves appeared on the windowsill, and then her friend and neighbor Jennifer's mom pulled herself into the room.

"Beauty?" she said. "You've been in here all this time?"

It was Jennifer, not Jennifer's mom, Beauty realized. How long had she been asleep? Jennifer cut the umbilical cords with her pruning shears, swaddled the babies in the slips from the pillows—girl in a map of the lakes, boy in a map of the rivers.

"Sleeping curses," Beauty said. "Man, what the fuck?"

A piece of string was tied round her finger, but Beauty could not remember what she'd wanted to remember when she'd tied the knot twenty-three years before. Now she wore the string ring in hopes she'd recall the cause of the babies as a night of passion with someone she liked. The twins got bigger every day.

The deputy sheriff who served the eviction notice was someone she'd been in band with in high school, skinny then, fat now. "You played alto, right?" she asked from the window.

"Yes. Come get this." He waved the document.

"Climb the tree and bring it, lard-ass," she told him.

He wrapped the notice around a rock and threw it but missed the window.

Beauty found the Chevy behind the castle, under a tarp weighted down with bricks, the Impala in which she'd learned to parallel park and French kiss. It turned over as if she'd been asleep a single night, not twenty-odd years. She strapped the babies into secondhand car seats Jennifer had given her and headed for the pediatrician's, listening to sports radio. She'd missed several generations of baseball stars.

When she went to the bank after the doctor's, she was told the piles of gold coins her father deposited when she was a teen-ager had over the years given birth to more coins while they slumbered. The teller winked, and Beauty realized she'd become a laughingstock, the stuck-up girl who claimed she'd been asleep when she got knocked up. She pushed the double stroller down the street, and everyone she passed was smirking.

She wanted a split-level in a neighborhood where no one knew her or the twins. Realtors showed her plywood-and-housewrap luxury townhouses between the pizzeria and the tracks, an abandoned multistory driving range beside the interstate that had great potential. When she thought it couldn't get any worse, one of them took her to see her childhood home. Quartz countertops, six-burner stove, bamboo floors, beige paint on every wall, sod where once the old queen had tended an herb garden—Beauty wanted to wail like the babies. The young king showed up just as they were leaving. Around her finger the string felt suddenly tight. Beauty saw him start, knew at once he was the father of the daughter and the son she held, knew he knew she knew. "You knew it would break the spell?"

"Well, no," he admitted.

It would've been easy to marry him—he asked right there and then in the driveway. Easy to pretend the long sleep hadn't been a curse but a blessing—solitude without loneliness, what could've been drab decades of life leapfrogged. Easy even to pretend it was love. She said no. She touched the string. Thin memories of sunrise and set, moon and rain and snow, framed by the high window.

THE PARROT

She was an only child, with no brothers or sisters, nor did she have any playmates. So they made her a doll the same size as herself, with a face and clothes exactly like her own. Everywhere she went the doll went too. At school her teachers and classmates treated the doll as if it were a real child, an eleven-year-old twin cheerier and more polite than the girl. The doll was a better speller and reader. On the playground the doll was a daredevil on the swings, while the girl worried about broken bones and looking like a loser. At home her parents got divorced, and nothing changed except neither wore a wedding ring. The girl found in the Goodwill box in the garage a self-help book that suggested children be given a nice gift before the divorce was announced—thus the doll, she figured. It was never moody or disrespectful, and it never complained about what was put on its plate at dinner. At school Kenny stopped paying attention to her and started paying attention to the doll. It was spirit week, and the girl made a point of wearing black leggings and a dark-brown T-shirt on Crazee Colors Day, but the doll dressed like a freaking *clown*—so much for matching. The girl cheated on the spelling test, got a better score than the doll, watched the teacher frown at the doll. After dinner the doll came into the rumpus room with a puzzled look on its face. It'd walked in on Mom and Dad. The girl attempted to explain the basics of sex. The doll looked even more puzzled. "How?" it asked, and the girl fetched from the Goodwill box *The Joy of Sex,* which one of her parents had hidden in a cookbook dust jacket. The doll flipped pages, asked, "Does Kenny know about this?" The girl saw the doll tap its crotch, blank as if someone had erased from it what the book pictured. The next morning she dressed in the PJs Day outfit the doll had laid out for itself the night before (bathrobe, pajamas patterned with the faces of cats, fuzzy slippers). Without comment the doll put on the drab daytime clothes the girl handed it. At school the girl grinned at Kenny, and he grinned at her. The doll sulked in homeroom, stuttered when asked in language arts to read aloud from *Moby-Dick:* "There is a wuh-wuh-wisdom that is woe; but there is a woe that is muh-muh-madness." They were walking home when a dark sedan pulled up beside them and a fat man said, "Your mother told me to come and get you. There's been an accident." The doll opened the door and got in, but the girl bolted—she'd seen the filmstrip about strangers in cars every year since kindergarten. She pretended she didn't know where the doll had gotten off to. Her parents stapled flyers onto telephone poles, the doll's face smiling blankly beside Xeroxed snapshots of lost dogs and cats. The girl imagined the pervert's disappointment and laughed. "Are you the doll?" her mother asked. In her voice was both worry and hope.

THE SLEEPING QUEEN

Our wives are to blame, to blame for the babies, first and foremost, because once upon a time there were no babies in our quiet, orderly, clean houses, but then our wives were delivered of our babies, therefore our wives are also to blame for the minivans and the comparative poverty and the disorder and the noise because our babies are to blame for the minivans and the comparative poverty and the disorder and the noise, and our wives are to blame for our babies. Our babies are to blame for making us worry about school districts, the rising cost of college, climate change, teen pregnancy, binge drinking—thanks a lot, babies—and our wives are to blame for our babies.

Our fathers-in-law are to blame for calling to the sides of their deathbeds our wives (younger, before we met them), to offer for the most part useless advice and then theatrically to breathe their lasts, convincing our wives most men are dopes and therefore making them irresistible to us when we met while enrolled in colleges, the likes of which we are now unable to afford to send our babies without second mortgages. There's nothing to be gained in discussing what our mothers-in-law are to blame for—nothing at all to be gained, trust us—and even less to be gained in claiming blameless our mothers.

Our wives are to blame for our passable table manners, which have helped us advance in our careers (software engineer, tenured poet, orthopedic surgeon) and have thus ensured we'll never again spend a sunny Wednesday morning reading for fun outside a coffeehouse next to a Laundromat where all our clothes save those we're wearing are in one 75¢ dryer, wondering if our not-yet-wives will tonight finally succumb to our clumsy seductions, then marry us, then teach us to eat with our mouths closed and our napkins across our laps.

Our wives are to blame for magic: Onto our fingers they slipped golden rings inscribed with their names, names so lovely they sound like synonyms for *sunshine, kindness, beauty,* then they gave us our babies, each baby wild and mysterious as a talking fox. Spring is here, the trees full of fragrant flowers. Our wives are to blame.

CANNELORA

And the same day even the bed gave birth to a little bed, the wardrobe to a little wardrobe, the coffer to a little coffer, and the table to a little table. The woman pushing the empty double stroller through the neighborhood with good schools and low property taxes gave birth to a little woman pushing a little empty double stroller, and the McMansion they were passing gave birth to a little McMansion, which crushed the brick rancher next door. Every recycling bin on the curb for Thursday pickup gave birth to a little recycling bin—and the beer bottles gave birth to little beer bottles, the coupon circulars to little coupon circulars, the flattened plastic seltzer bottles to little flattened seltzer bottles, and the broken-down Amazon Prime boxes to little broken-down Amazon Prime boxes.

The folklorist from the women's college who was walking her bichon gave birth to a little folklorist from the women's college, and her bichon gave birth to a little bichon. The big and little folklorists stooped to pick up bichon poop in biodegradable bags, the little bichon's poop little, the little folklorist's biodegradable bag little.

At the elementary school, while the kids were out screaming on the playground, the dissected cow's eye gave birth to a little dissected cow's eye, the pencil sharpeners to little pencil sharpeners, the boxes of crayons to little boxes of crayons, the desks to little desks, the drinking fountains to little drinking fountains, the library books to little library books, the stacks of bubbled-in Scantron sheets to little stacks of little bubbled-in Scantron sheets. The WPA era elementary school was too old to give birth, so the teachers and the little teachers had to herd their students and their little students into rooms that'd been overcrowded to begin with and were now piled with crayons and little crayons, compasses and little compasses, secular inspirational posters and little secular inspirational posters.

And the same day even the trees gave birth to little trees, the birds to little birds, the clouds to little clouds, the breeze to a little breeze, and the sun to a little sun.

Animal Locomotion

Hayseeds in high collars, Franklin Cobb and his fraternity brothers boarded the train in Atlanta, bound for Chicago and its Columbian Exhibition, each embarrassed into sullenness by his excitement. They seated themselves in the smoking car and puffed comically large cigars they bought from a boy on the platform, then hassled a porter for a pitcher of water and seven glasses. When the train jerked to a start, each sipped his water and dumbly watched Atlanta flashing in the windows. Soon the view changed from progress and hubbub to pine scrub and clapboard shacks, the young men's tongues were loosened, and they set to abusing Cobb.

"It's twenty dollars for *each* of us," said towheaded Samuel.

"Yep, it'll be twenty dollars each." Cobb pointed to his pals one by one: "Twenty, forty, sixty, eighty, one hundred, one hundred and *twenty*."

In his cups the day before, Franklin had vowed to find a wife at the Exhibition, and his friends had suggested a friendly wager.

◆ ◆ ◆

She was in love with the naked man who did the backflip. Each morning on her way to A Street in Cairo, Ruth paid her penny and entered the Zoöpraxographical Hall to watch him tumble. She had never seen a man out of his clothes, and the sight amazed her every time. Mr. Muybridge or one of his assistants lectured on animal locomotion as the man sprang backward, but Ruth did not hear a word. Between the man's legs was the penis, and every day her cheeks flushed at the sight of it. His ribs looked like a piano's keys, and she imagined putting her fingers on them.

She left when a galloping horse replaced the man. A minaret poked the sky, and she walked to it, young men already waiting in line to pay a nickel to watch the danse du ventre.

◆ ◆ ◆

One of the boys from Georgia had a sheet of instructions for Exhibition visitors he'd cut from a newspaper, and they followed its dictates. They spent the night seven to a room to save money, rose before the sun, and set out at dawn to make the most of the day. They took a cab to the foot of Van Buren Street and paid twenty-five cents to board the whaleback steamboat. Admission to the Exhibition was fifty cents. Franklin's friends stood at the end of the pier complaining about the cost, but he was thrilled to have already spent the better part of a dollar. It made him feel reckless, cosmopolitan. He bought an apple.

The early-morning crowds were thin around the huge turbines displayed in the Machinery Hall, but as the hours passed, more and more people joined the young men in their gawking.

In the Electricity Building an Egyptian Temple glowed mysteriously, each hieroglyph luminous in the dark. They walked through the Mammoth Crystal Cave in the Horticulture Building and through the aquarium in the Fisheries Building that made Cobb feel he was underwater. On the Wooded Island in the Lagoon they stood dumbfounded before the buildings of the Japanese Ho-o-den. Along the South Pond dozens of windmills stood like huge metal flowers. Cobb and his friends sat below them and ate their lunches.

◆ ◆ ◆

Ruth was sickened by the obscene notes wrapped around the pennies they threw violently at her while she danced, but there was no other way, save doing what the notes demanded, that she could pay for her room and send money back to her mother. Her hair was black and thick, her skin darker than that of the Irishwomen in her rooming house. No one at the Exhibition noticed she was Italian, not Arab. Her first job at A Street in Cairo had been to sell mineral water to the leering men. On a lark she had learned the belly dance from Little Egypt, a true Arab with an earring in her nose, and one morning when Little Egypt did not arrive, Ruth became her. She thought of a cousin who wrote her letters while she danced—until she saw Muybridge's show, after which she thought of the naked man.

◆ ◆ ◆

Cobb and his pals paid a dime to see Hagenbeck's Animal Show. Lions rode horses, and tigers rode velocipedes. In the Zoöpraxographical Hall they watched moving pictures of a man laying bricks, two men fighting with swords, a mother spanking her child. Ferris's wheel was fifty cents, and Cobb's friends refused the price. Franklin went alone into the car and took a chair by the window, rising slowly above the Exhibition. Domes and cupolas and spires grew skyward; tiny trains followed tiny tracks, and tiny gondolas floated along tiny canals. Smoke came from stacks and snapped like banners. In all the excitement he'd forgotten his wager, but alone in a crowd of strangers, he remembered the vow. He looked at the little ladies far below and wondered which he would wed.

They were exhausted when they reached A Street in Cairo. The boy with the page of instructions realized with a gasp they had viewed in one day what should have taken five. Defeated, they sat on chairs they paid a penny to rent, drank strong, sweet coffee, and watched children enjoying camel rides. "Time for the hootchy-cootchy dance, gentlemen," a man in a bowler called from a doorway. A queue quickly formed, and Cobb and his friends joined it.

◆ ◆ ◆

The boy was born ten months later. When he was old enough to ask, his mother smiled and told him, "I was a belly dancer in Cairo. Your father wrapped a note around a dollar and rolled the coin to my feet. The note read, *Will you marry me?* I mistook him for a man I loved and agreed." The child knew she was fibbing: Cairo was in Egypt, and Egypt was in Africa, and his mother was from the part of the map that looked like a lady's boot, and his father had never traveled farther than Georgia to Chicago.

Black Cat

Remember prom, boutonniere pressed flat during slow dances as if it'd been preserved in a book. Remember heat radiating through rented pants, through creaking tulle skirts, more than the heat of first sex. Remember blood on the sheet, the twitch of pleasure that shook her. Remember college, Saturday nights becoming Sunday mornings, coffee and the *Post* in bed, comics and front page kicked to the floor, sliding and crashing like water. Remember the breakup. Remember hours of pool with physics major sharps who could not lose. Remember running into her at Sibbie's Halloween party senior year. Remember being naked in the Honda in the parking lot, rain like code on the roof, windows fogging, then glowing as dawn broke. Remember reconciling and having to eat two Thanksgiving dinners, one with her parents, one with yours. Remember the Christmas tree blown into the middle of the street in which the black cat played. Remember laughing at her while she stood at the second-story window clad only in a blanket, conversing in Spanish with Mormons, too polite to ignore the bell. Remember driving away to

Baton Rouge, long lists of vows trailing. Remember the second breakup soon thereafter. Remember sadness and loneliness like possessions taking up space in the room. Remember your birthday falling on Thanksgiving, the trip north, how she gave herself like a gift. Remember Christmas. Remember the night in February she begged to be taken back, and you, standing barefoot on the tiny rusted landing, looking at the alley's luminous shell gravel and listening to her voice being pulled thin by a thousand miles of telephone wire, sure that prospects for love were numerous in that weird city, said no.

Memento Mori

After you die, you keep living in the same apartment. Your grand-mother moves in and serves you course after course of bizarre food—wasp in aspic, sticky pink noodles that taste like cotton candy, popsicles made of cheap wine, brown bread from a can. Your mail keeps coming, but it's nothing but oil-and-lube come-ons offered in what appear to be Japanese characters. Suddenly you can read what appear to be Japanese characters. Every night you dream about dying. All of your favorite novels turn into pop-up books—*Moby-Dick* is really good. One digit of your phone number rolls up, one down, and the vinyl siding people call every morning. A man you briefly dated becomes the star of a stupid sitcom that quickly goes into syndication and is offered twice nightly on the only station your TV brings in.

Those Dogs

My daughter is married to a kindhearted boy who loves dogs. Into their home he brings dogs no one will adopt from the shelter where he volunteers, unlovable mutts old and cranky or young and not house-trained as well as an alarming variety of abused purebreds. Sometimes there are a dozen dogs in their modest ranch house; once there were nineteen. Some end up adopted by someone else, some die, but all those dogs are quickly replaced. Too many dogs if you ask me, but I'm not asked, and so I keep this opinion to myself. The smell cannot be ignored. The dogs are all ugly. When it became clear this wasn't some altruistic phase her husband was going through and there would always be a pack of defective dogs living in my daughter's house, I wondered what was wrong with her—didn't she comprehend how nuts it was to have that many dogs, all of them fucked-up? Then I worried her husband married her and loves her because like the dogs my daughter is defective, is kin to skittish inbreds who can't hold their piss when the doorbell rings. Then I wondered if it was my fault she's so. It's painful to see the dogs whose puppy collars have been left to tighten around their necks as they mature, cutting into their skin, leaving collars of scars. Or maybe my daughter's not broken, but the problem is that for some reason I can't look at her and her sweet husband and their weird happiness and think simply and honestly, *Good for them and for those dogs.*

The Great War

Open the book, and a smaller book pops up. Its red cover is stamped with a gilt title too small to read—could it be French? The smaller book is on a thin-legged desk that stands on a Turkish rug before a tall, narrow window hung with simple curtains. Outside there is a maple tree with an octagonal trunk. All this popped up when the small red book popped up, but it is the book you noticed. The curtains are yellow. They lift as if touched by a summer breeze. The leaves of the maple shiver and show their pale undersides. A cloud the dull silver of an old nickel has risen and unfolded while you marveled at the curtains and the tree. A knife of lightning stabs the maple. Lines of rain slant from the cloud and come across the sash to soak the book. Its pages become wavy and thick with moisture, and the book opens like a fan. Sammy's brother left the window open, and Sammy's book is ruined.

Turn the page, and the book and the window and the thunderhead fold away and a forest of charred stumps rises from pocked mud. A boardwalk snakes between the stumps. Its planks are gray, crosshatched with a wide grain and marked by outsized nailheads. You hear the boom of cannon and the crack of rifles. There is the smell of gunpowder and burning rubbish. Three doughboys walk along the boardwalk singing a nursery rhyme. Sammy is the last in this short line. The soldiers' arms and legs are nearly round, but if you look closely, you can see where they fold when they have to lie flat.

Turn the page, and two aeroplanes rise toward each other, rattle their guns, pass so close each pilot can hear the other's curses—English from the Sopwith's cockpit, German from the Fokker's—and dive toward the lush paper grass of the mountain meadow. Below the dogfight Sammy and the two other dough-boys—David from Kansas and Richard from Boston—sit on the grass. They tear a long loaf of bread into thirds, pass a canteen of wine, wipe their mouths with the backs of their hands. Above the picnic the red triplane and the moth-brown biplane rise and dive, rise and dive. A patch of wildflowers pops up, and Sammy picks a bouquet and offers it to Richard. Richard pretends to be a girl, and David pretends to be Richard's jealous beau. A squadron of yellow butterflies jerkily crosses the meadow while the doughboys wrestle and laugh. Sammy pins David, and Richard kisses the victor. Above them a shock of orange fire unfolds to engulf the Sopwith's tail.

Turn the page, and the landscape leaps up at you, broken trees and a bombed-out barn. The jagged wound of the trench crosses both pages. A voice from beyond the knotted wire of no-man's-land calls, *Wine for tobacco? Wine for tobacco?* No moon jumps into the sky. Sammy watches over David's shoulder while David zips the pages of a dog-eared flipbook, animating the coupling of a naked man and woman. From the German trench again comes the offer to trade wine for tobacco, and again the doughboys ignore it. The knee-deep water is scabbed with ice, and it trembles when a shell screams over the trench and lands off its mark. David drops his flipbook into the water and curses. Richard, who had been too prudish to look, laughs. Both their mouths are very dark, giving away the truth that they are hollow inside. A flare lights above the trench like a bulb hung on a cord. Sammy looks down and sees a torn photograph of someone's sweetheart floating on the dirty water. The gas alarm sounds, and Sammy and David don their masks. Richard hunts in his rucksack and cannot find his. David pulls off his mask and puts it over Richard's face, unbuttons his pants and pisses onto his handkerchief, covers his mouth and nose with the urine-soaked rag, and screws shut his eyes.

Turn the page, and the war flattens under the weight of a victory parade. Red, white, and blue bunting hangs from lampposts. Children ride their fathers' shoulders. A brass band plays and an organ grinder turns his crank and his monkey dances a stiff jig. Soldiers march in formation, legs parting and closing like scissors. Sammy is in the middle, a head taller than the rest, so you can easily find him. A gang of wiseacres breaks rank and unfolds a banner that reads NO BEER, NO WAR STORIES. A girl in a calico dress darts into the street and kisses one of the soldiers on his cheek. Close the book, keeping your finger between the pages to mark your place, and when you open it again, you will see that she chooses a different soldier. Open and close it until she picks Sammy.

Turn the page, and a house snaps up at the head of a flagstone walk, its windows bright with light. Do you recognize the maple? Each room is illuminated just long enough for one detail to be seen—Brother's baseball mitt, Father's pipe, Mother's sewing machine, Sammy's ruined book.

Turn the page, and a table pops up from the floor. You can smell baked apples. Mother and Father and Brother and Sammy pop up too, napkins in their laps. Father carves the ham, a brown cone marked with black grid. You hear laughter, the music of forks and knives on the good china. A banner on the wall reads WELCOME HOME! Mother covers her face with her napkin and weeps for joy, a silent tear slides down Father's cheek and hangs on the tip of his folded nose, and Sammy chews with his mouth open.

Turn the page, and the small book pops up once again, the gold words on its red cover still too tiny to read. The desk, the window, and the maple rise as well. Sammy stands at the desk in striped pajamas and looks out the window. The pages below wink with fireflies. A cloud slides across the flat circle of the moon, dimming the room and Sammy's face for a moment. The curtains rise and are then pulled out the window, where they wave stiffly. Over and over Sammy tries to close the waterlogged book. Each time it pops open again. His chest fills and empties with a creaking sigh. He shakes his head and licks his lips with his paper tongue. Bats hunt bugs above the pages of the lawn. The book he holds becomes the book you hold, open to the pages of the victory parade, and Sammy watches the girl in the calico dress dart into the street and kiss his cheek.

Quilligan

She came in at one a.m. reading to her mother from a paperback *Slaughterhouse-Five*. "He had a whistle he wasn't going to show anybody until he got promoted to corporal" made her mother chuckle, but "He had a dirty picture of a woman attempting sexual intercourse with a Shetland pony" got silence. It was the summer of New Coke and Madonna in *Penthouse,* the summer joining my junior year of high school to my senior, and I was working third shift at 7-Eleven. Past midnight seemed an odd time for them to be in the store, but that neighborhood of Volvo station wagons and swimming pools was not mine. She was in sweats and a shiny soccer jersey striped dark green and chartreuse, and she wore a calico bandana over her hair like a religious girl. I guessed she was fifteen, a year younger than me and the age I'd been when I read *Slaughterhouse* so many times that I immediately knew where she was in the book.

From the store's far corner, her mother fetched the miniature shopping cart I'd never seen used, and they began going up and down the narrow aisles. In the security mirrors mounted high in the shop's corners, I watched her boy's butt and memorized the name printed in white across her shoulders—*Quilligan*. I'd been taught very little before being left alone in the store from eleven to seven, but one thing I remembered from a training video was that late-night grocery shoppers were suspicious. Cigarettes and condoms and Slurpees were the biggest sellers in the dark single-digit morning hours. Anyone who browsed was dangerous. For a moment I thought of the chart over the toilet that identified different guns—*semiautomatic, shotgun, revolver*—so you could tell the police what had been pointed into your face.

Her voice stopped, and in one of the convex mirrors her bent reflection licked the tip of a finger and turned a page. I imagined calling her Quilligan, like she was a guy, imagined she'd call me Balk, that this would be our joke, no baby talk or nicknames from the Smurfs. "His head was tilted back and his nostrils were flaring," she said. "He was like a poet in the Parthenon." She read carefully, her voice pure as a radio DJ's. Her mother filled the little cart with fruit cocktail, pork and beans, *Cosmopolitan*, Kraft Macaroni & Cheese. They passed close to where I stood behind the register and the drop safe and went down the chips, housewares, batteries, and school supplies aisle. Her ears were not pierced. A strand of brown hair was looped around one.

I watched her mouth as she read and imagined her lips moving like that when we kissed. I imagined her crossing her arms, holding the bottom of her striped jersey, and pulling it up over her head. Her armpits would be hairy like Madonna's. Her bra would be white and plain, and she would close her eyes when I worked its clasp. I'd never kissed a girl who moved her lips, and no girl had ever taken off her shirt in front of me.

Her jersey had a big 9 on the back. "It was New Year's Eve, and

Billy was disgracefully drunk at a party where everybody was in optometry or married to an optometrist." Her mother giggled, and Quilligan joined with the same giggle, hers lower in pitch. When she bent to her book, I saw the calico knot tied under her ponytail and wanted to kiss it and then kiss the knots of her spine. She kept reading while her mother chose a gallon of milk from which only an hour earlier I'd done as my manager instructed and erased a passed expiration date.

They came to the counter, and she read, "He was in the back seat of his car, which was why he couldn't find the steering wheel," while I rang up their groceries. "I love that book," I told her, and they looked up at me as if they'd been sitting in their living room and heard a stick snap below their window. I am twice the sixteen years old I was that night, and I still see the fright in Quilligan's suddenly tight lips. When they pushed open the door and fled, the top of her lowered head was just inside the orange five-feet-from-the-floor section of the marker I'd been taught to check so I could report how tall the criminal had been.

Verso

The USA's too new for Baedeker's legends of cathedrals built atop mosques built atop temples. The closest we come are TV shows and movies about what happens when a subdivision or 7-Eleven or parking lot is built over a Native American burial ground. In Denver I tried to find daguerreotypes in antique stores and was told no one in Colorado circa 1840 was allowed the vanity of having her portrait made. Even our oldest cities are all surface, our visions of their evolutions just visions of our aging selves we see flashing in their shop windows and puddles. The city of the last night with one lover and the city of the first night with another, the city of leaving in what feels like defeat and the city of returning in what feels like triumph, the city of madness and the city of sanity: it's a single city. On the verso of an old postcard a message written in a fin-de-siècle hand fades to sepia, while the recto shows a landscape unchanged.

LPs

My father can't remember where a lot of his LPs came from. He insists they must be mine, abandoned when thirty-odd years ago I left for college, but these are not my records: *At Folsom Prison, Sgt. Pepper's Lonely Hearts Club Band, Lou Reed Live,* Coltrane, Jefferson Airplane, Little Richard. "Maybe one of your friends gave you these," I suggest. "Friends?" he asks, like he doesn't recognize the word. Meanwhile, my son is pricing the albums on eBay. He keeps sighing at his phone: Everything's selling for five dollars. I remember several covers from my childhood—Dylan's *Basement Tapes,* Dave Brubeck wearing a turban and holding an armload of Pan Am carry-on totes—but cannot recall ever listening to any of these records. That was before eBay. Back then it was just my opinion that anything my parents liked was pretty much worthless, and therefore my time was better spent listening to tapes of Big Country and "Rapper's Delight" in my room. My son chirps excitedly, then groans. "This would be three hundred if it was an earlier pressing and not torn up." He shows us *Bo Diddley Is a . . . Lover,* edge ripped by long-dead cat King George. "Remember when Lori Dorfmeister's dad found that Elvis 45 in the box at the yard sale and you let him have it for a quarter?" I ask my father. "That must be worth a lot now." He stares at me and says, "Yard sale?" Later, driving away from my forgetful father's apartment, I will explain to my son that moment at the yard sale was the first time I remember being embarrassed by my dad. Lori's dad asked him if he really wanted to sell the single for "two bits," and my father, too cool to admit he didn't, took the man's dollar bill and made change, big fake smiles on both their faces. My son will ask what song it had been—*I don't know.* Had there been a sleeve—*no.* Had it been a first pressing—*I don't know.* Then he'll tap his phone and tell me I could be describing a record now worth perhaps five dollars, maybe five hundred, but probably just five. And for some reason I'll think about my oldest memory, the time I almost fell down a well. One summer day when I was no more than four, my parents took me to the farmhouse of some hippie friends, and while they all drank beer and talked, on a wooden stage just my size I stomped a circle and flapped my elbows like a chicken until suddenly the boards snapped and I dropped and my outstretched arms stopped me and I felt below cold nothing and my father ran across the yard yelling my name and pulled me up into his arms.

Eleven Stories

TANGERINES

It was the winter tangerines were absurdly cheap, and so we all walked with our jacket pockets full of fruit. When we gathered at the café, we ate them with the harsh espresso that we cut with hot water. I had a room in the Latin Quarter when the Latin Quarter was still dangerous and exotic—knife fights and old ladies in mantillas. The walls were thin and a family with a sick baby lived beside me, and when it cried and struggled for breath in the middle of the night, I would rise from bed and pace the room with my blanket wrapped about me worrying as if it were my child, my breath visible in the cold. Its mother's voice was clear and beautiful, and I had to fight the desire to press my ear to the plaster to listen to her calm the child. I would light an egg of coal dust in my stove, hating myself for wasting fuel, then peel tangerines and squeeze their skins over the fire. Small blue flames hissed above the orange glow of the coal while the woman sang to the baby. I never saw her and one day there was a sign offering the room, but it was not odd for people to come and go in the Latin Quarter. Waking with the baby had become such habit that for weeks I paced the floor. Soon tangerines were again unattainably expensive.

THE VILLAIN

A boy we mostly ignored claimed he had done something horrible he could not confess because we would despise him if we knew. None of us believed him: He had slim wrists and played chess. Paul laughed at the boy and called him "The Villain" until the boy begged Paul to guess his crime. "Forgery?" Paul taunted. "Mail fraud?" The boy made his hands into fists and pursed his pretty mouth into a knot. That night it snowed, and in the morning the city was white. The girl who delivered the cakes told us the boy had stabbed a tourist with a sharpened screwdriver in front of the cathedral just past daybreak. The blood, she reported, looked beautiful on the snow until you realized what you were seeing. For weeks Paul would not speak to us. He sat before a game of chess he was playing with his brother through the mail. He made his move, wrote it on the back of a picture postcard, waited for his brother's response. The boy appeared one morning with a deep-blue bruise on his cheek. The wound had been minor and the assault his first crime.

THUNDER

At noon the radio told us it was the coldest day on record, but what held our attention was the thunder sounding while the snow fell—we were children during the war, and we remember the bombs. Paul and I went to a saloon in the Polish Quarter and squandered our coins on pachinko, the thunder obscured by the rattle of the silver balls falling peg by peg.

VERONICA

I won a raffle and bought a ticket to travel south to the town in which my mother was born and then felt generous and asked Paul if he wanted to join me. I made much of the veronica kept in a stone church just outside the village and the famous tree from which traitors had been hanged, and he agreed to come along. The train trip was long and uncomfortable, and we were both exhausted by the time it was over. I bought sandwiches from a boy and had him wrap them in paper so we could have a picnic. It was sunny and warm. Paul made us hats from folded newspaper. We rented bicycles at the depot and rode beside a clear creek whose bottom was marked by the reptilian pattern of sunlight falling through moving water. I could not find the church with the veronica, and Paul got angry. Night came, and I refused to pay for a room. We lay under our coats on benches on the depot platform and waited for the first train of the morning. A radio played through a speaker horn.

POSTCARD

Jonathan died in sunny June, but a postcard he sent me in May did not come until September. I read the message about his trip to Rome and the novel he read on the train and dressed quickly and walked to his favorite secondhand bookshop. The shop had three copies of the novel he praised, and in each I tried to find the question marks and exclamation points I remembered him writing in the margins when we would sit and read under the ginkgo in the garden behind his kitchen: I'd been told by his sister that Jonathan's mother had sold his books to this shop when he died. In one of the copies a heart pierced by a dagger was drawn in pencil on the flyleaf and a Latin motto was written below it.

MOTHS

A girl I liked the look of made raku bowls and sold them in the open-air market in the Polish Quarter. One day I bought a small one without even looking closely at it just so I could touch her when I handed her my coins. In the café I showed the bowl to Paul and only then saw it was painted with a pattern of moths.

DOPPELGÄNGER

The boy who had stabbed the tourist with the screwdriver came to the café early one evening. Since his weeks in jail, he had begun to frequent a criminals' café, and we rarely saw him. When he found me playing tic-tac-toe with the mailman, he smiled. "I knew it was a lie," he said. "The paper says you were arrested for beating a man." We found the police blotter in the evening edition, and the boy showed me my name. "What does this mean?" I asked. The boy shrugged. "Be kind and find out what's going on," the mailman said in a father's voice. The boy looked as if he'd been waiting for someone to ask him to do just that. Paul and the mailman tried to calm me while the boy was gone, but I could not stop reading the notice of my crime. "A man named Jakub Kidd took your wallet in the bathhouse this morning," the boy reported an hour later. I touched my pocket like a fool. "When he was arrested, he showed your identification papers and claimed to be you so his pension wouldn't be revoked. He was a trolley driver before the rails were torn up in the riots, and he gets a half-salary from the city." The boy had me turn my head. "From the side he looks a lot like you." The mailman bought the boy a stick of candy and thanked him for helping. Paul and I found Kidd in the city directory. He wife was Ana and his mother-in-law Gerta Schmidt. His address was in the

Latin Quarter. "If I were you, I would go and live the bastard's life to right the scales," Paul told me.

MISPLACED

One morning in the middle of winter, it was suddenly spring. Warm breezes made the ribbons in the hair of schoolgirls snap and flutter, and the sun burned the snow from the rooftops and from under the dark evergreens in the formal gardens. In the mean park in the Polish Quarter bright birds appeared and bulbs groaned in the dirt. The streets were filled with children tossing balls and old people on the arms of their adult sons. The windows of the café were thrown open, and we sat stunned behind our cups. None of us said it aloud, but we all knew the misplaced season could not last, and none of us was surprised when the cold and the snow returned at dusk.

THE BATH

Friday mornings I went to the open-air market to pretend to buy fruit so I could smile at the girl who sold raku bowls. She had begun to recognize me and return my smile, but I was still startled when she spoke to me. "I don't really know you, but I'm going to ask for a favor," she said. "I live above a tobacco shop, and the owner's gone away for the holidays. He turned off the heat when he left, and the pipes have frozen. I can't bathe or wash my clothes. Do you have a tub?" I nodded even though I did not. For a dollar my neighbor would let me bathe in his, and I was willing to pay for the girl to have a bath. I wrote my address on a scrap of paper, and she told me she would be along as soon as she sold one more bowl or when it began to get dark. A block away I gave two little boys enough money to buy the bowl and have that much left over and made them promise they would not swindle me. I rushed home and lit the stove and put some bread and fruit on a plate. She did not mention the lie I had told when I led her up two flights of stairs and paid the pensioner to let her use his bathtub. I waited in the hall chewing my thumb. When he opened the door, the sour old man was grinning and the girl was laughing as if they had just shared a good joke. A towel was wrapped about her head. She wore a flannel nightdress and carried her clean, wet clothes in a tin bowl. On the stairs she said, "He gave me his daughter's gown—she's dead." I hung the wet clothes over the stove, and drops of water fell from them and snapped and jumped on the hot surface. The room was warm, and the windows had fogged from the stove's heat and were lit orange by the falling sun. The girl walked around the edge of the room eating cheese and looking at the postcards I had tacked up like little paintings. When she found the bowl painted with moths on the sill, she turned to me and said, "I forgot you bought this." She sat beside me on the rug before the stove and put her feet where they could get warm. Her toenails were jaggedly trimmed. She did not speak when I took her feet into my hands. As I remember it, she stood and took off the robe and for a moment she was nude and I was dressed and sitting on the floor with my hands in my lap, but when we were joking later, she recalled my hands had jerked the buttons from their holes and she had been unable to resist my advances.

THE MOON

The rain froze and covered the city in glass. Paul and I walked and looked through the ice at the rubbish frozen in the gutters.

From a pushcart we bought sweet potatoes and used them to warm our hands until they cooled enough to eat. Paul pointed to a sparrow killed by the ice—it still clung to a twig, its wings extended. In the park in the Polish Quarter, the moon was a kite tangled in the topmost branches of a tree.

SPRING

The bowl with the pattern of moths was on the sill, and when I touched it, the moths rose and fluttered against the frosted glass. The panes were clear when I woke, and I knew winter was truly over.

Truck Tire outside Murfreesboro, Tennessee, 1936

A retread's lost reptilian hide fools him. In the dark Walker takes it for a road-killed gator and pulls the Ford over to investigate. Forehead against the cool curve of the steering wheel, he realizes what a double fool he is. No alligator lives thirty miles south of Nashville, and the girl he's told to meet him in Georgia doesn't deserve jilting. He considers the tire, illuminated by the head-lamps, so he won't have to consider the girl. Its tail curls off into the ditch. Beyond it is country darkness.

He rubs his nose and smells her. He hasn't washed his hands, and even the perfume of breakfast's bacon cannot cover that smell. He closes his eyes and sees the picture he took of her while she sat on a bench in Coliseum Park, plaid school skirt hiding her knees. A week later that same skirt was folded neatly on a chair when he took a picture of her naked and smiling on his bed—he sees that picture too.

There'd been idle talk on the subject of the institution of marriage. His face white with Burma Shave, her father chased him down Royal Street brandishing a pair of barber's shears, yelling "Evans! Goddamn it, I'll *stick* you!" Walker wrote the address of a rooming house in Valdosta on the back of a postcard and told her he'd see her there. The address was a fiction. He had no idea if Valdosta held an Oleander Street.

The tire, he reminds himself, the tire that looks like an alligator, and when he glances up, he sees the last light drain from the headlamps. Dark silence when he turns the key. Cicadas ratchet mockingly. The coffee he's sipped from a vacuum bottle to fight off sleep begins to fail him. He lights a match to check his watch and is spooked by the reflection of the small flame in the side mirror. It's past midnight, hours until any filling station will open, and he has no idea how long the walk to the nearest will be.

The blanket he wraps around himself smells like New Orleans—mildew and whiskey and gasoline. Walker shifts on the seat and can't find comfort. The darkness is the same with his eyes open or closed, and pictures he's made of the girl appear either way. He sees her in a line of girls in plaid skirts waiting at the window of a snowball stand, sees her asleep in a chair, feet on the windowsill, sees her cooking eggs wearing only his undershirt.

A tire that looks like an alligator, he tells himself. *The pines skinny and at their bases bound to one another with blackberry bush barbed wire. The ditch calico with wildflowers. A filling station with a Nehi sign nailed over a broken window.*

House

If Roebuck's were crowded and noisy on a Tuesday night, maybe I could think about something other than how I should be at home confessing to my wife I got laid off before lunch, but it's just me and another guy three stools down, and the bartender has the Hawks game turned to a mumble, so all I can do is feel guilty for pretending I'm out having a beer with someone I hated in high school.

The layoff shouldn't have surprised me—the university's cutting is never-ending—but I thought the Middle Eastern Institute was small enough to escape. Turns out a half-time administrative assistant (me) and a photocopier lease are enough to warrant zeroing out. It didn't help when last week a peckerwood legislator called a press conference and singled out the Institute's budget and a queer studies professor's salary as two examples of taxpayer monies squandered in ways un-American. If Kim gets reclassified to half-time, which might happen, since books, too, are clearly a waste of monies, we'll have no monies for health insurance, no monies to support six-year-old Hazel and our forthcoming baby, no monies to pay the mortgage.

I should be at home reading want ads, editing my résumé, looking up temp services. Instead, I'm pretending I'm hanging out with someone I haven't spoken to for more than twenty-five years, not since we were seniors in suburban D.C. Facebook was where I learned he, too, ended up in Atlanta. His profile proved that the only thing we'd ever had or would ever have in common was being seventeen at the same time, in the same zip code, but tonight I need a bullet-pointed list of "career objectives" that makes me appear to be someone other than a forty-three-year-old who's been working part-time for six years while taking care of his kid and trying to become again an artist, and I couldn't bring myself to admit this need to Kim, so I told her I was meeting Brett for a beer.

The bar's other customer is wearing painter's whites and sipping a longneck High Life. Cigarettes and sunburn and a mustache flecked with beige semigloss make it hard to tell if he's twenty-five or fifty. We watch the Hawks lose, the news comes on, and the face of the jailed child rapist looks a lot like my face. The anchorwoman details the pedophile's crimes, and in the mirror behind the bottles I see disgust twist my mouth and narrow my eyes until I look even more like the squinting pervert in the mug shot—and I watch the housepainter's reflection note the resemblance. He looks back and forth from the TV above the bar to me, limps over, and throws a slow-motion roundhouse I have no problem ducking.

The bartender sounds bored when he says "Out" to the boozer.

"But—" the drunk protests, pointing to the TV.

The news has moved on: Alpharetta apartment fire, surveillance camera footage of a junior high school bus beat-down out in Morrow.

The painter mutters, "Aw, hell," picks up his Marlboros, and leaves.

"The fuck was that?" the bartender asks.

I shrug, relieved I don't have to convince him I'm not a child molester.

The weatherman smiles: blue skies and highs in the middle fifties all week.

The bartender asks, "Another?"

I shouldn't—I've had two already—but I'm unemployed and lying to my wife, and I feel the need to prove I'm a normal guy, the painter's drunk and crazy, there's no reason for him to take a swing at me, so I nod, and he pours pint number three.

I worry the news will circle back to the pervert, so I drink quickly, pay my tab, and stumble out into a disappointingly tepid January evening. I'd hoped for sobering cold. There's no sign of the housepainter, but I look over my shoulder every few steps as I walk past my car and down the block to the coffeehouse. Tuesday night in Little Five Points, and it's just me and the young woman behind the counter. I order a double espresso, sit by the window, dump three sugars into the demitasse, watch the traffic light change from green to yellow to red, think about being laid off, think about being mistaken for someone who rapes children, think how sick are people who rape children—then make myself think about high school.

I wonder if Brett's still jealous about Emily. She and I were together the summer between my junior and senior years, when

I worked at the 7-Eleven in her neighborhood. I lived on the other side of the school district, and though we knew each other from band—she played clarinet, I played tuba—she was a year younger, and I'd never talked to her much. I clerked graveyard, eleven to seven, and one morning at about five thirty, after I'd spent another long lonely night reading *Penthouse Letters,* a car pulled up, and Emily got out from the passenger's side. She wore a Caps jersey and sweatpants, and I could tell she was half-asleep. She went down the candy aisle to the milk cooler, lifted a gallon of skim, and headed back toward me with her eyes on the ground, flip-flops smacking her heels. When she put the milk on the counter, I said, "Hey, Emily."

She jumped as if the jug had spoken, looked up at me, then smiled. "Carl, right?"

A horn honked. Her mother waved impatiently.

I slept through the day, then went back to work, and just after midnight she walked into the lot, but instead of a hockey jersey and sweats, she wore a Fishbone T-shirt and madras Bermudas. I was surprised to see her, surprised when it turned out she'd come to see me, surprised when she came back the next night, then the next. I wasn't supposed to allow anyone to hang out, but I let her stay for as long as she would, and sometimes she was with me for hours. Her parents were divorced—her father lived in Richmond, and her mother was out of town for work more than she was home. Emily's neighborhood was the kind a sixteen-year-old girl could wander alone in the middle of the night and where only two weeks later that girl and a boy could, an hour before the boy's shift began, make out on a bench in the tiny, dark park tucked between the decommissioned firehouse and the branch library.

Emily told me *No boys in the house* was pretty much the only rule she and her older sister, Patty, had to follow while their mom was away. She claimed it was to keep from Patty's bed whichever boy she was dating. That July and August the boy was Brett, and they found plenty of other places. Emily was, like me, a virgin, and we sanctimoniously agreed we didn't need condoms and Slurpees topped off with Bacardi like Patty and Brett, swore it was thrilling enough to progress in two weeks from talking when I was supposed to be stocking sodas to heavy petting in the pocket park before I clocked in. Her sister and Brett parked in the darkest corner of the 7-Eleven lot, and we rolled our eyes though only hours before I'd had a hand under Emily's bra.

Sanctimony's short-lived when you're sixteen and seventeen. A friend and his family went on vacation, and he gave me the key to his house so I could feed the cat. Emily and I nervously joked about which bed we'd do it in—*Too soft! Too hard! Just right!*—before agreeing on my friend's older brother's futon because of all the options it had the cleanest sheets. For a couple weeks after, we halfheartedly had sex in my parents' car, on my back porch, once in the stockroom at 7-Eleven while a sign on the locked store door told customers I'd be back soon. Sometimes, while we dutifully moved against each other, I'd see on her face a look of pinched concentration I worried I, too, wore. We were both trying to feel again the thrills we'd felt on the park bench, something I understood when once we did it with our shirts on and all I could think about was the night in the park she unbuttoned her sundress and for the first time I saw her breasts, luminous in diffused street light.

Her mother returned from a business trip to Seattle, and Emily stopped coming to 7-Eleven. I felt stupid when I realized

I didn't know her phone number. When I called information, the operator told me it was unlisted. Brett came in one night and informed me Emily, Patty, and their mom had gone to Hilton Head for a vacation. He grinned and shook his head and said, "Man, Patty'll do *anything*, but you got the ass I really want." I pretended I didn't know what he was talking about.

Fall semester began, and the smile Emily gave me when I saw her in band and the cafeteria was the smile you give someone who's never seen you naked.

I use a tiny spoon to scoop sugar-and-coffee goo from the bottom of the little cup. The first time I saw them, Emily's nipples were bigger and darker than I'd expected. After being mistaken for a child molester, I've been thinking about a sixteen-year-old's nipples, her pubic hair, the faces she made. "I was *seventeen*," I remind myself aloud—and wonder if I'm okay to drive.

When I go to the counter to order a second *doppio*, the barista frowns at me. I try to convince myself all young women with hair dyed Kool-Aid blue who work at coffeehouses frown at every tipsy, jobless, middle-aged man who talks to himself, but I can't win the argument. "Did you see that thing on TV?"

"I don't *own* a television," she brags, and I'm relieved she finds me generally uncool rather than specifically disgusting.

Back at my table by the window I try to think of the polyester 7-Eleven uniform shirt I should've stolen but instead returned to avoid a ten-dollar fine, but I can't stop thinking about Emily's underwear, so I close my eyes and think about the first time I saw my wife's underwear, our second date.

We met at FSU—Kim was about to finish a master's in library science, I was about to drop out of the visual arts MFA program after a single disappointing year—and on our first date coffee led to dinner led to the bar led to her apartment, and there she mixed gin and diet tonic. We ignored our drinks while we kissed on the couch, slowly listing toward lying down, each of us keeping a foot on the floor to maintain propriety. She held the back of my neck to keep my mouth pressed to hers and kept kissing me when I eased my hand under her shirt and over her ribs and onto her left breast, but when I moved it to her right, she let go of my neck, untangled her leg from mine, stood up, and said nervously, "Too quick."

I assumed that was the end of everything, but two Fridays later she called and asked if I wanted to get dinner, and after dinner she invited me back to her place and poured me a Tanqueray and diet Schweppes. She seemed disappointed as I sat sipping my sour cocktail. I thought she wanted me to leave, so I did. Standing outside her apartment, looking down at the shopping cart sunk in the deep end of the glowing blue swimming pool, I considered the way she'd smiled when she offered me a gin and *diet* tonic, just like the time before, and how she'd looked puzzled when I drank mine while hers sat untouched on the counter. I knocked, she was grinning when she opened the door, and we went directly to her bedroom. Her panties were black lace. When I eased them down, I was amazed to find her hairless, a novelty in '95.

I spent the night and then the next night and then the next. A week into our cohabitation, she asked if my crotch itched. That's when she admitted she'd shaved in an attempt to rid herself of pubic lice, a failed attempt, as we both could feel. Her ex—they'd dated for a semester at UGA five years earlier—had been in town, and she now seriously regretted what she'd considered harmless nostalgia sex.

She said she assumed I understood how it's easy to sleep with someone you've slept with before, how it makes you remember when things were simpler, when you didn't worry so much about so many things, and how it's especially easy if someone never hurt you back then and so, stupidly, you trust him.

"You think I'm a slut, right?"

What I thought was I wanted to be with her, even if she'd given me crabs.

"I'll never hurt you," I swore.

She looked taken aback, and I worried I'd again gone too far too fast, but her face softened, and she said, "Good."

Kim's black lace underwear, I tell myself, finish my coffee feeling proud of thinking about having sex with my wife, and then feel guilty for spending almost forty dollars on three beers and two coffees rather than heading home and telling her I've been laid off. We still joke that if we could tough out pubic lice when we barely knew each other, our relationship can survive any challenge: marriage, underwater mortgage, parenthood, flirtatious coworker, dead parent. I hope we can make it through lost job and financial ruin.

Maybe that's why I started thinking about Emily. For a few minutes I distracted myself with memories from a time when things were simpler, when everything—most notably sex and heartache—was new and seemed at once amazing and unremarkable. Thinking like this convinces me I'm sober enough to drive.

The Honda rattles as it warms. Hazel won't go to sleep until I get home. Sometimes it takes only a single page of a favorite book before she drops off, but I have to be the one reading the page, which means she's been up later than normal on a school night and will therefore lose sleep—and here's another reason to feel guilty.

Through the murky windshield I watch the housepainter who tried to punch me weave along the sidewalk toward the car. I turn off the noisy defroster and hope he keeps his eyes on his shoes. He passes, veering away from the curb and toward a closed barbershop, and I let loose the breath I hadn't known I'd been holding—but then his face is pressed against the passenger window and he's pounding the glass and screaming, "*You sick motherfucker!*"

When I pull away, he falls into the street, still yelling. I'm looking in the rearview more than where I'm driving, and I almost go through a red light. "The guy's in *jail,*" I say out loud, as if I need to remind myself why the drunk's accusation is bogus. Do I look to him not just like a specific child molester but like someone who molests children?

Child molesters are one of the many things I worry about more since Hazel was born, along with money, rape, school districts, antibiotics in the milk, razor blades and needles in Halloween apples. Fatherhood's introduced me to fears I never knew when single or even when it was just me and Kim, which probably proves I'm not the feminist I'd like to believe I've always been, but at least now I'm that feminist, maybe, hopefully. Turning onto my street, I have a horror movie vision of the door kicked in, blood on the wall, my family dead. My hands are shaking on the wheel when I pull into the driveway. The door's closed, the curtains bright with secure lamplight. When I look to make sure the FOR SALE sign's in the yard, a greasy ghost of the painter's face smeared on the Civic's window spooks me.

The clock on the stove: 9:47. Kim's alone in the living room reading *Harry Potter*. She rests the open book on her pregnant belly and smiles. I walk over and sit beside her. When I put my hand on her knee, it stops shaking.

"Hazel's asleep?" I whisper.

"Playing Barbies. Waiting for you to read her something. You have a good time with Whatshisname?"

"Brett. Asshole when we were in school and still an asshole." I should tell her I've been laid off, a drunk tried to punch me. "Did you see that thing on TV?"

"Nasty."

My hand jerks on her knee. "Nasty?"

"The state can't afford an expansion of Medicaid that'll help half a million poor people, but we can afford to pay for a billionaire's football stadium?"

She's talking politics and professional sports, thank God. "Bullshit," I agree.

Hazel clops into the room wearing a pair of Kim's loafers over her sneakers. "Daddy, want to see my danth?" she lisps— and it occurs to me I've spent the Tooth Fairy's five-dollar bill on coffee and now have no cash for Hazel's second front tooth, lost at lunch at school.

"Heck yeah," I say, hoping Kim's got folding money.

Hazel stomps furiously and over the racket hollers, "Oh! Hard to get old! Oh! Hard to be young!" a song she made up this afternoon in the car on the way home from a playdate at her friend Zelda's.

We clap, and Kim says, "Amen, sister. Time for bed."

Hazel bows deeply and pounds down the hallway.

adulthood

Now's the time to admit I've been laid off. "Hey," I say, "I have to tell you some—"

"*Daddy!*" Hazel screams from her bedroom.

Kim yells, "No yelling!" and shuts her eyes. They're still closed when she asks, "What were you saying?"

Hazel hisses "*Daddy*" in a stage whisper.

I've lost my nerve. "Tell you later."

Coffee's made me three-quarters sober, wide awake, and needing the toilet. I poke my head into Hazel's room and say, "I have to use the potty. Right back."

After I brought her home from Zelda's, Kim took Hazel to the Y to swim. Their bathing suits hang over the shower rod. Kim saved the faded one-piece from when she was pregnant with Hazel, evidence that six years ago she was somewhat less than sincere when she claimed there absolutely wouldn't be a second child. It's a generic black Speedo, and every time I see it, I think about the black Speedo she wore the febrile first week we were together, before the crabs hatched.

Past midnight that week's Wednesday, both of us buzzed on gin and diet tonic, I stood atop the shopping cart in the pool's deep end with Kim's legs wrapped around my waist. Perched there, the water was thigh-high. Though the pool lights were off and the courtyard only dimly lit by bug bulbs burning over a couple of the dozen doors that opened onto it, making out on what was basically a stage was exciting, even if it was late—or early—enough for an audience to be unlikely. Kim kissed my ear, and I hooked my fingers into the crotch of her Speedo and pulled it aside, feeling her stubble on my knuckles. Her feet slapped the surface of the water behind me when we started.

She bent to bite my shoulder, and over her head I saw crouched in the dark beside a chaise lounge the not-yet-teenaged boy I'd seen on other nights messing around in the parking lot when kids his age should've been asleep. I watched him watch us, and then Kim grunted and startled me, and I stumbled off the edge of the cart, taking her into the deep. We came up gasping and laughing. The kid was gone, and instead of feeling annoyed or embarrassed, I felt generous, as if we'd shown him something more beautiful than the versions I'd seen in magazines when his age—but a twelve-year-old boy doesn't see beauty when he spies on people doing it atop a Piggly Wiggly buggy in an apartment complex pool, or if he does, he sees the same beauty in *Hustler*. Did I want to see people having sex when I was twelve? Yes, but that doesn't mean at age twenty-five it was right for me to feel generous because I didn't stop screwing my girlfriend when I saw him watching. I never told Kim about that kid, and I never will.

Raspy yapping from next door: Happy Al, the neighbor's pug, out to pee.

When I stand and look down, the bowl's filled with blood, proof I've been right to fear the skin cancer removed from the back of my knee last year sent a taproot to my colon before the dermatologist hacked it out—wait, beets, I ate beets at lunch. To keep myself from mooning over cancer, mooning that'll lead to sadness (three friends lost, one each to brain, lung, and colon) and fear (soon I'll have no health insurance), I tell myself when my son's born, my bowel movements will move down from third to fourth in importance in the family, a pathetic thought to have in order not to mourn or worry.

"Daddy!" Hazel hollers.

"No yelling," Kim shouts from the living room.

Hazel has a pile of books ready beside her on the bed. Last week she and I made an attempt to thin her library so it would fit on a single set of shelves and thus open up space for the crib. The house has only two bedrooms, and when he gets old enough to leave ours, she and her brother will share—one reason I'd hoped we could sell and find a habitable, affordable three-bedroom in the same school district, hopes now clearly vain and foolish. It'll be a miracle if I can pay next month's mortgage. Thinning failed. Every title's too important to lose. I know her hoarding is because even before he's born, the baby is splitting our heretofore undivided attentions, but there's no room for his bed. We've compromised: I'll read every book to her before she has to decide what goes to Goodwill.

I open *My Cat Can Bake a Cake,* a board book once Hazel's favorite. Some nights she made me read it over and over and over. "Eggs and butter, flour and milk." Those repeated nights mean now I don't have to think about the story as the cat greases the pan and preheats his potbellied stove, and my mind starts to wander back to the night in the pool. Turning the page of *My Cat Can Bake a Cake* reminds me I'm sitting beside my six-year-old daughter while thinking about having sex with her mother while a child watched. I concentrate on the cat's batter.

Hazel's eyes are wide. "I can read thith," she lisps, then corrects herself: "This. *Stir it once, stir it twice, stir it three times and it will taste nice.*" The hissing S's caused by not having front teeth to tap with her tongue make her sound like she's three again—when I used to read her this book—and I feel one of those *My-little-girl-is-growing-up* heartaches, the severity of which always surprises.

"You can read books way harder than this one," I proudly remind her.

"When I was a baby and you used to read thith—*this*—to me, I didn't know what words were."

"You can read it to your brother."

The suggestion delights her.

I hear Kim's phone ringing as Hazel continues: "*Into the pan, and you lick the spoon. Into the oven, your cake's baked soon.*" While my daughter describes the cat icing what turns out to be a birthday cake for a dog, I decide I'll tell Kim I've been laid off as soon as Hazel's asleep.

"Carl?" Kim calls. "Come here?"

"Read this next." I tap the cover of a book about a dragonfly who doesn't want to take a bath.

Kim's hunting in Hazel's backpack, cell pressed between ear and shoulder.

"What's up?" If she weren't on the phone, I'd tell her now—I really would.

"It's Natalie. Zelda's Barbie shoe collection is missing, and Hazel's the last one Zelda saw playing with them."

"Barbie shoe collection?"

"I'm too tired to interrogate her. Find the shoes, please."

When I walk into her room, Hazel hides something under her pillow. "Do you have Zelda's shoes?"

"No." She's a bad liar, but she doesn't seem to be lying—and then I understand.

"Do you have Zelda's *doll's* shoes?"

She nods. I expect two or three pairs of tiny heels, but what Hazel's hidden under a pile of stuffed animals in the corner of the room is a purple plastic pill case big as a book. There are twenty-eight compartments—Monday to Sunday multiplied by Morning, Noontime, Evening, and Bedtime—and each compartment holds two pairs of miniature shoes.

Hazel fusses, "She has *ten* Barbies already, and she got *three* more for her birthday, and I only have *eight*. It's not fair."

I'm too dumbfounded by the sight of the shoes to ask if it's fair she has eight Barbies while most of the world's children have none. "Stealing is bad," I instruct instead. "Bad people steal." I leave Hazel to consider this and take the box to Kim.

"March," she says when I come back to the living room. "But if he doesn't stop with the elbows, I'm not letting him stay in there much longer." I hold up the pill case. "We've got it. Carl'll bring it to school in the morning. Sorry, Natalie."

After she hangs up, I shake my head. "Who buys her kid fifty-odd pairs of Barbie shoes?"

Kim opens the box and seems to be counting. "Whose kid steals fifty-odd pairs of Barbie shoes?"

I almost ask if she's got five dollars for the Tooth Fairy but can't, then wonder how I'll tell her I've got no job if I can't manage to admit I've spent the Fairy's money on coffee.

"*Daddy!*" Hazel shrieks.

"Don't yell!" I yell.

Again she hides something under her pillow when I come back, but I don't demand to see what because I worry she's pilfered more than Barbie's shoes, and I want to maintain Hazel's blameless. To blame is Zelda's mother's poor parenting, her bourgeois foolishness. Indignation keeps me focused, and all I think about as I read board books with Hazel is what a good, smart, generous kid she is and how rotten the world can be: selfish, greedy, stupid, bigoted, filled with plastic crap. She falls asleep, I wait until her breathing slows and evens, and then I ease my hand under her pillow to find what she's hidden: *My Cat Can Bake a Cake*, a sealed envelope with her tooth inside, the Sharpie she's used to address the envelope to the Tooth Fairy and to add three exclamation points to the book's title and to every sentence. *My Cat Can Bake a Cake!!! Eggs and butter, flour and milk!!!* The corners of the cardboard covers are soft from hundreds of readings, love no novel ever suffers. I turn the thick pages and consider how she's made new with punctuation what's little more than a *Cat in the Hat* rip-off. The hat of the cake-baking cat is yellow with green stars, but he looks familiar enough, and the stars are obviously supposed to make me think of Sneetches, and I wonder how the publisher avoided a lawsuit. Then again, can any children's book cat after Seuss's not be a reference to the Dr.'s? Hazel snores at this deep thought. I turn off the light, and above us luminescent stars stuck to the ceiling glow pale green.

I need to tell Kim I've been laid off. I look up at the stars, and as I do off and on, I fear Kim's having an affair. Usually I can reason with myself this worry's silly, but being jobless and lying to my wife about it, and two coffees and three beers, and being mistaken for a pervert, and having Hazel steal a bunch of tiny shoes, make it impossible for me to be reasonable.

In the living room, when I sit down beside her, Kim winces, and I wince too. "He's been kicking all day, nonstop," she says, then grimaces, and then grimaces even more dramatically and holds her side. "Hazel never did this to me."

She's exhausted. It would be cruel to tell her. This, I know, is bullshit.

"Never again," she vows, again. "What was I thinking?"

She heads to bed. It's ten thirty, and there's but one beer in the fridge. I open it and hope I can drink myself calm. The case filled with shoes is on the coffee table, and I have the urge to put a handful in my mouth and wash them down like a suicide would pills. Set on end, the case looks like a purple plastic Joseph Cornell box. Kim isn't having an affair, I know. Worry begat that worry, and I'm worried. Fretting over a drunk's fixation is silly, but I can't sell my house for anywhere near what I owe the bank, my wife's going to have a baby in two months, and because of state budget cuts, I'm unemployed and soon she might be too. Less worrisome, therefore, somehow, to believe she's sleeping with a fellow librarian.

I go to the kitchen, hoping I've overlooked another beer, but I haven't. There's a bottle of kid's cold medicine on the countertop, seal broken, miniature measuring cup sticky. Hazel's nose has been running, but she hasn't been coughing, and we'd agreed not to give her medicine. Obviously, Kim changed her mind. I find the dosage chart on the bottle and check the plastic cup's graduations. Hazel weighs forty-four pounds, meaning Kim should've given her two teaspoons, but there's purple residue up to the 3.5 mark. I worry Hazel's been overdosed and has died. As quietly as I can, I hurry to her bedside. In the weak illumination of her nightlight, I cannot detect the rise or fall of her covers, and just as I'm sure she's not breathing, she moans and starts grinding her teeth. When I told the dentist about the grinding at Hazel's last appointment, she breezily dismissed my concern by reminding me these were baby teeth, which made me sure Hazel would crack her permanent teeth as soon as they grew in.

I know I should trust Kim wouldn't accidentally kill our child, but this pregnancy's made her absentminded. Carrying Hazel didn't, and I wonder if that's because worry made her alert, and now that she knows what's normal and not, she doesn't worry as much—and I wonder if the reason I worry now is then I was too ignorant to worry. When I told her I was more nervous about this baby than I'd been about Hazel, she joked, "The novelty of diaper changes will be gone," and when I responded, near panic, "But . . . the *penis*," she laughed so hard she had to lean against the wall.

Hazel's teeth squeak. When she has nightmares, I have to climb into her narrow bed and sleep with her. Her bad dreams are infrequent, but once or twice a month one comes to her around three o'clock, high time for weird shadows. I'm feeling like I've started awake from a nightmare—hard to tell what's real and what's fear—and for a moment consider bunking with Hazel to make myself feel better, then think of the housepainter and the molester on the news. I check the floor beside Hazel's bed for sharp toys and find only plush animals. I need to find five dollars.

There's a twenty in Kim's wallet, what's left of the forty dollars she got from the ATM before church. As it does every Sunday, twenty went into the collection plate. The remaining twenty is her coffee allowance, untouched, perhaps because her lover's paid for her decaf two days running or because she's frugal and drinks herbal tea at her desk. I'm going to have to borrow five singles from Hazel's piggybank, which means waiting until she's deeply asleep.

I get the laptop and open Facebook and think to look at Brett's friends and in so doing find Patty and Emily, and the mystery of why I haven't before been able to find them is solved: Patty's now Patty Patel, and Emily's Emily Duncan.

Emily's a social worker, divorced, has kids, ten and eight, both boys, lives in Newark, Delaware, and is remarried—I'm weirdly delighted to see—to someone named Jessica. I consider a message, a friend request, but decide that's a bad idea. I look at snapshots of her boys playing soccer, of Jessica gardening, of Emily carving a jack-o'-lantern. She's not sixteen anymore, and seeing proof of this in photographs of her on the beach wearing a black Speedo one-piece calms me for a moment, then has me thinking about sex again, which perhaps is a godsend since the other things to think about are bloody shit and no health insurance, real estate bubbles and school districts, unemployment and child molesters.

Do I always think about sex this much, and has the housepainter's mistake made me notice, or has his mistake made me think about Emily specifically and sex generally more than normal—and what's normal? What percentage of my thoughts should be about something other than past sex? Should my brain be tasked only to worry about money and to keep me breathing?

When I try not to think of Emily, I think of Dianne, the girl I met in Michigan the summer after Emily, the summer my family vacationed in the U.P. When a few months later I bragged about her to my freshman roommate, he mocked, "You wouldn't know her—she's from Canada." I had a postcard with a breezy message and a canceled stamp that proved she was real and lived in Toronto, even if it didn't prove we'd had sex twice, but I didn't show it to him because his laughter made me worry I'd imagined her moving slowly atop me, smiling, the tent's roof bright at noontime when everyone else was safely off canoeing. My roommate superglued a tiny Canadian flag on our door, and for the entire year I had to look at the maple leaf whenever I came back from class or the library or a weekend visiting my parents.

I can't remember Dianne's surname, but I remember my roommate's. I haven't thought about Jim in years, but Facebook finds him: he's in D.C., working for CNN. Winthrop—Dianne's last name. Either she's not on Facebook, or she, too, has a new last name, or Jim was right and I made up a Canadian girlfriend, conjured from lust and a dumb joke a name and hips and breasts larger and softer than Emily's. And here I am again, thinking about a teenager's boobs.

The password for my university email account still works, which shouldn't surprise me: Ralph, my boss, a Comp Lit professor, mastermind of the Middle Eastern Institute, was shamefaced when he told me I'd need to come back tomorrow to sign some paperwork since HR didn't finish processing my severance in a timely fashion. There's a message from the athletic department inviting everyone to the catered press conference where they'll welcome the new coach for the horrible football team— hundreds of thousands of dollars wasted on catering, the coach, and crappy football. I delete without opening another message, this one urging me to buy season tickets using my faculty/staff discount.

Hazel's orthopedist has reminded me the final follow-up is tomorrow afternoon. In September, Hazel went off the side of a slide and snapped her humerus. We spent a night at Children's, and the next morning a surgeon put two pins in her arm. The hospital bill totaled $6,754.50, but we were responsible for only the $75 copay. When, six weeks later, I took her to have X-rays and the pins removed, I paid another $25. Thursday there will be more X-rays, and the grand total will reach $125. If Kim's reclassified to 49 percent and we have no insurance, the next broken arm or malignant lump on the back of my knee will bankrupt us. I consider retrieving the season tickets email from the trash and composing a rant to the stooge who sent it about Hazel's broken arm and what a joke it is that the university affords a losing football team by screwing over librarians and secretaries—a stooge who will never get laid off because she or he works for the football team. Maybe it's better to think about sex.

When I log in to Gmail, there's a robot message from Arts Assets reminding me that I haven't finished my grant application and that the 15 January deadline is looming. The grants are small, $1,500 to $3,000, but losing my job means I can't keep taking classes for free, and I'm only six thesis hours from finishing my MFA. Three thousand dollars would almost cover the cost of those last hours—or serve as the down payment for a visit to the ER or the dermatologist. I click the link and jump to their website. The artist's statement must be no more than four hundred words long, and already I'm in the high three hundreds.

Several years ago my wife and I went to London at Christmastime to celebrate our tenth wedding anniversary. When one morning my wife woke up hungover and told me she wanted to sleep off her headache, I went alone to the Tate Modern. The Turbine Hall was filled with Rachel Whiteread's Embankment, *and standing amid those fourteen thousand stacked white boxes I was convinced, once and for all, I wasn't an artist. Depressed and overwhelmed, I followed fellow tourists into galleries filled with yet more proof I'd been fooling my-*

self: Duchamp's Fountain, *Giacometti's* Walking Woman, *a Cornell box. I stood under a Calder mobile and watched its shadow moving on the floor. That shadow made me think of other shadows: the shadow of a good time that comes in the form of a hangover, the shadows of dead friends. When an elderly couple innocently walked across the shadow, I cringed as if they were stomping on Calder's sculpture. On my way out I was again dwarfed by* Embankment, *but at that point all I could think about was that shadow. In the gift shop I bought a Calder postcard, drew below the picture of* Mobile *a version of the shadow I'd seen on the floor, wrote on the back, "Sometimes the shadow's more beautiful than the thing that casts the shadow," and pretty much stopped making art. Two years later I found that postcard in a novel I had bought to read on the plane, and something lined up in my brain: the shadows cast by Cy Twombly and John Baldessari and Rachel Whiteread and Bruce Nauman and Duchamp and Calder and Joseph Cornell and Dorothea Tanning weren't engulfing me; rather, they were giving me infinite material to work with. It was at that point that I started the project* Shadow [X]. *The first* Shadow *was cast by Calder. I built a half-size model of the mobile that had been in the Tate, hung it, and lighted it so that it casts a shadow like the one I saw in London:* Shadow [Mobile]. *Since then I have created Shadows of works by Rachel Whiteread* (Shadow [House]), *Joseph Beuys* (Shadow [How to Explain Pictures to a Dead Hare]), *and the Philistines who in the Book of Samuel are told to cast golden rats and "emerods" as offerings to stop plagues of rodents and hemorrhoids* (Shadow [1 Samuel 6]). *For each* Shadow [X] *I construct a*

*model of the original artwork and light it so that I can create
a recognizable shadow, then move the light as sunlight would
move, creating a kinetic image. Support from Arts Assets will
allow me to continue to expand this series.*

I'm not going to be any smarter tomorrow than I am tonight,
even if I'm soberer, and if I leave this undone, it's going to make
me more frantic than I already am. I make sure my phone number and email address are correct and click SUBMIT.

Matt was sicker than I knew when I told him my idea for
Shadow [X]. I went back to Tallahassee to see him before I'd
thought to build the Calder model, and I was sitting beside what
would be, in a few weeks, his deathbed when I showed him
the postcard from the Tate with the drawing of the shadow. He
shook his head and grinned. "A *shadow?* Brilliant—seriously. I
wish I wasn't going to die so soon so I could spend more time
being jealous, maybe steal the idea." The sadness I feel when I
think of Matt is unlike any other I feel for lost but living friends
or lovers, and of course that's because he's dead, not just lost
to time or moving or growing up or getting married or having
kids, and of course it has something to do with the feverish
moment in my life when I met him—and nearly simultaneously
met Kim and dropped out of graduate school—but I wonder
if the pain is still sharp because he was the first person to die
whom I cared for deeply and took for granted would always be
around to complain to me and to listen to me complain.

Someone laughs outside. It sounds like he's on the porch, but
when I peek out, I see a kid on the sidewalk, phone pressed to
his ear. It's probably my neighbor's son from down the block—

he's the right height and skinny like that teenager—but he's wearing a balaclava knit to look like a Mexican wrestler's mask, so even though he's standing under a streetlight, I can't be sure.

The FOR SALE sign's a little billboard on which is advertised my desperation: *Price Reduced.* Tomorrow morning I should send Hazel out there with her Sharpie to add exclamation points. There was only one showing in December, and Brenda the realtor didn't make an appointment. I walked home from dropping off Hazel at a playdate to find Brenda in her car at the curb, thumbing a text message, oblivious to everything else. I assumed she was waiting for someone, and I hurried in to tidy. In the bedroom I found a guy my age closing my sock drawer. The pillows had been flipped—he was looking for guns. "Only one bathroom?" was his lame attempt to pretend he wasn't. All I could manage to say was "Totally redone." I should've thrown him out, not let him act like the lack of a half-bath made the house uninhabitable. I should've yelled at the agent, called her boss. Instead, I followed the guy into the kitchen and bit my tongue when he insulted Kim's choice of yellow, didn't tattle on Brenda, told her I hoped to hear from her soon.

There's no way we'll get back what we paid for 193 Grove Road, let alone what we've put into it: HVAC, roof, plumbing, kitchen cabinets and countertops, the $3,000 bathroom renovation my parents paid for. It's on the market because last June a developer bought the abandoned triplex next door and put up a sign in the yard featuring an architect's rendering of the generic four-bedroom, five-bath he'd build anyone willing to give him $650,000. He'd paid $90,000 for the place, I knew, and it seemed logical we'd easily get $200,000 for the bungalow for which we owed the bank $130,000. Brenda agreed, and the two of us began browbeating Kim. When Kim claimed there was no way we could afford to buy a bigger house in the school district, even if we cleared $60,000 in profit, my counterargument was that there was no way we could afford the emotional costs of living in a tiny house with Hazel and a baby—this was September, and she was already showing. I was a jerk, Kim gave up, and we put our house on the market. Then the developer figured out the triplex, like our house, sits on the edge of a floodplain and therefore he can't build anything that doesn't match its circa 1958 ranch house footprint, a footprint on which no four-bedroom, 3,500-square-foot house can sit unless it's four stories tall, which is against code. Again the place is abandoned. Its gutters hang off, and squirrels and raccoons live in its attic. No one wants to pay $197,500 to live next to that. No one wants to pay $197,500 for a backyard that's squishy after a gentle rain.

The kid on the sidewalk laughs into his phone again. A minivan with skateboard stickers all over its side stops to pick him up.

I go out the carport door because it squeaks less. Even before I caught the guy in my sock drawer, I knew I didn't want to move, didn't want to scold Hazel anymore for leaving clutter on her bedroom floor, as if being able to see her rug will magically cause someone to call Brenda and make an offer, didn't want to keep pretending to Kim I believe someone will call Brenda. I count the informational flyers in the plastic box attached to the FOR SALE sign—ten, one fewer than when I checked before I left for the bar—and then tear them all in half and put them in the trash, not recycling. The sign comes out of the yard with one tug, but I don't know what to do with it, and it belongs to Brenda, I guess. Maybe some other delusional dope wants to try to sell his house. Into the Honda it goes. I stand where the kid stood, in a puddle of yellow lamplight, look at my house without the sign, think about the nights when I was fourteen, fifteen, when I'd sneak out the basement door and walk my neighborhood feeling tough because I was on the streets after bedtime, then think about walking through Emily's neighborhood on the way to some dark spot where we'd have sex—tonight all the roads inside my head lead to sex, sex, sex. Do I have few friends because I've never outgrown my teenage lusts? Did the housepainter recognize this?

Hazel calls for me, which makes me feel needed and loved and panicked. Inside it's quiet. I imagined my daughter's voice. I sneak into her room and steal her piggy bank. In the hall I uncork it and pull five singles from the hole in its belly, replace the plug, sneak back in and put the pig back, and swap the money for the envelope with the tooth inside.

Agitation's loosened my bowels yet again, and I sit on the toilet trying to figure out which of Flaubert's sentences have led Kim to dog-ear pages in the translation of *Madame Bovary* she's left on the tank. On page 53 is she noting *"What a pathetic man! What a pathetic man!" she said softly, biting her lips,* or did she want to come back to *Spring returned. She had fits of breathlessness with the arrival of the first warm days, when the pear trees flowered?* I notice the gray ring around the tub. I flush and reach to pull up my pants and see the foot of pink curling ribbon Hazel tied to my backmost belt loop after school. Surely the housepainter, the bartender, and the barista saw it. I'm too old to feel like a fool, but I wonder if my pig's tail had something to do with the painter's certainty I'm a pervert.

Under the sink there's baking soda and a brush, and for five minutes all I need to think about is scrubbing off soap scum, making clean the place where my wife and daughter and I bathe, where soon I'll bathe my son. The sink's filthy, toilet's filthy, floor's filthy. The bathroom's my responsibility, and I've done a poor job keeping it hygienic. In the kitchen I fill the kettle and flip up the whistle on its spout so I don't wake anyone. By the time I've got the toilet scrubbed and the sink, mirror, and spigots gleaming, the kettle's rumbling. On my hands and knees on tile my mother and Kim chose, prettier and more modern than I would've picked, I knock loose grime from grout and crap from corners, including a knot of Eggroll's hair. The cat's been dead three months—wait, no, *four.* Her fur shouldn't be here. More evidence I've half-assed my responsibilities: I work part-time in order to keep the house clean—*worked* part-time. Dry mopped, the floor gleams. The room reeks of lemon verbena. I make sure *Madame Bovary*'s exactly where it was before.

I need a job, hopefully one with benefits, and if that means stocking shelves at Publix, that's what it means. Back on the couch with the laptop, I find the online want ads. In order to secure gainful employment, I need an MBA, a nursing license, a pharmacy license, three years of auto repair experience, five years of building-machine maintenance experience, an advanced understanding of PeopleSoft metadata, good enough credit to get financing to buy a Snap-on Tools franchise. I'm qualified to be a paralegal, I learn from an ad, and the thrill I get startles me. I click the APPLY button to see what I need to do. They want just a résumé, cover letter's optional, but if I'm qualified for this job, thousands are, the mob already uploading. I need a letter better than the one I can write in the middle of the night, I need sleep, I need to make sure my résumé has no typos, and I need to compose an argument making clear O'Sullivan & Norman would be foolish not to hire me.

A car door slams, and I peek. The minivan's back, and my neighbor's son is laughing as he gets out—he's not wearing his mask. It takes me a second to realize what's missing from the lawn is the FOR SALE sign that's been there for six months. I wonder if my neighbor's kid notices the absence, then he trips over his own feet and falls into my yard, still laughing. It's been a long time since I've been that high. I need to text Brenda and tell her to take the house off the market.

I know someone in HR at the university—Bill, who took a printmaking class I TA'd a few years ago—and though I cannot imagine they're hiring in the middle of the so-called budget crisis, I go to the Recruitment & Retention website. The Art Department's hiring a full-time administrative assistant.

Kim can quit her job before she's reclassified, before the baby's born, stay home with him and Hazel. I can be the breadwinner, get my MFA, go to the doctor's, take Hazel to the ER when she breaks her other arm. Now I'm awake enough to write a killer cover letter. I'm so jacked up I cannot help myself—I send Emily a quick hello and add how happy I am to see she's got kids and a partner.

I write Bill a note telling him I've seen the job posting and I'm interested in applying. When I click SEND, a batch of messages I haven't seen appears, some time-stamped as early as three o'clock.

There's one from Cedric, the custodian who empties the Middle Eastern Institute's trash, and it's formatted like a memo:

To: Carl Wilson

From: Cedric Greene

Re: Conversation on January 8

I want to tell you that your comments during our conversation on Tuesday, January 8, were not acceptable. You seem to
think that because I am black, you can yell at me. If you continue to harass me, I am going to file an official complaint.

I was angry after Ralph told me I'd been laid off, after I filled
a Kroger bag with my stuff and then went to use the little restroom across the hall from the Institute office. The urinal and the
floor beneath had been growing filthier and filthier for weeks,
and now there was a puddle of piss. For a few days I'd been able
to smell it from my desk, and twice I'd asked Cedric nicely if
he could do something about it, and twice he'd acted like I was
kidding by suggesting he do his job, like this was another in-
stance of the somewhat one-sided, somewhat good-natured
joking we'd been up to for months, almost ever since I started
at the Institute. He called me "Karl Marx" when I told him about
taking art classes for free, even though he's finishing his MBA
the same way I'm affording my MFA: a class at a time, snuck in
before or after work—or on the clock. The floor was so nasty I
couldn't bring myself to unzip. We'd chatted enough for me to
know Cedric put together LTDs and Tauruses at Atlanta Assem-
bly before Ford closed the plant and laid him off and that when
he finishes his MBA he hopes to work for Home Depot or Coke
or maybe even Ford, and I thought about this and about how I'd
been fired and about how I couldn't pee because the stink was
so bad. I found him down the hall, prying staples from a bulle-

tin board with a screwdriver, and I knew, from long experience doing the same kinds of invented tasks, that he was slacking, but now I had no job and he was pulling staples instead of doing his.

"The restroom floor needs to be mopped."

"I do floors on Friday," he lied.

"It needs to be mopped today—*it's your job.*"

He inhaled through his nose, let out a long sigh, said, "If the truth hurts, wear it," and went back to his staples, humming.

As I walked across campus with a shopping bag filled with desk gewgaws and pictures of Kim and Hazel in cheap frames, I wondered if it proved I was racist when I assumed he was intentionally mashing up clichés to mock me rather than making a mistake because if he was a white former autoworker pursuing an MBA while getting paid for not mopping floors and he'd said that, I'd assume he was an idiot, not a trickster or like a DJ—and isn't assuming a black person who mangles a cliché is a "trickster" or "like a DJ" proof of my prejudices?

He's cc'd Ralph, and there goes my brief macho fantasy of Kim before the ironing board, pressing a shirt for me to wear to my full-time job in the Art Department, the baby and Hazel at the breakfast table, laughing cherubim with faces plump from my paychecks. I'd finish my MFA, adjunct a class or two on the side, maybe get hired to teach half-time, then full-time. Cedric makes it sound like I'm an angry bigot, and no university would let an angry bigot be a professor or even an administrative assistant. I didn't think telling him to mop the floor had anything to do with race, but he did, and maybe he's right.

I consider trying to salvage things with an apology, including a note about how one of my best friends in college was black— Ann, who died from a brain tumor, whom I turned down when once she asked if I wanted her to spend the night (my black girlfriend, to go with the Canadian), but what if I turned her down because she was black, and what if the reason she asked was because the tumor was messing up her brain? And for fuck's sake, he's angry because I told him he should mop the floor because I was angry because I got laid off. If I punch the wall, I'll have to fix the hole—float sheetrock, match the paint—and probably go to the emergency room. If I send a message to Cedric suggesting he screw himself, I'll prove he's right, and if I send an apology and cc Ralph, I'll prove he's right, and if I do nothing, I'll prove he's right.

The laptop chimes. Emily's responded. *Fun to hear from you! Hope you're doing well! Can you tell me how to make it so not everybody can see my pictures?* She doesn't need my help; already I can no longer see her on the beach. *Do you know Emily?* Facebook wonders. Maybe the only thing we ever had or would ever have in common was being young at the same time, in the same zip code—and sex, which had more to do with proximity and being tired of waiting to become adults and believing sex would move us out of childhood than it had to do with anything that would last twenty-six years.

There's nothing to do but upload my résumé for the paralegal job and pray. When I go back to the newspaper to get to the want ads, the top story is now about the child rapist for whom I was mistaken. In Talbotton, down south, while his sister was off getting pizza for lunch, he molested two little girls she was supposed to be watching.

Hazel sobs, "Daddy!" and I bolt for her room. She's standing on her bed, her normal reaction to nightmares—get away from the pillow. "I was having a dream."

"It's okay," I soothe, thinking *alligators, sharks, being left behind.*

"Is Spain in France?"

"No, those are two different countries."

She nods, lies down and pulls the covers up to her ears, and is instantly asleep. I'd like to get into her bed, pretend she needs me there to scare off what's frightened her, but she wasn't afraid, just thinking in her sleep, therefore my urge is selfish—and isn't perversion selfishness taken to an extreme? I need to apply to be a paralegal.

The mug shot is not a mirror. His eyes are brown, mine are blue. There's a scar under his eye, while I'm unmarked. His hair's straight, and I've got curls. He's five foot nine, and I'm six even. My résumé's saved as a PDF, and he's in jail in Talbot County (not the first time, says the article). I upload it to the law firm's HR portal and then turn off the machine.

In the cabinet high above the cereal boxes where we keep our medicine so Hazel couldn't get it when she was two and her little brother won't be able to either, I find my Seroquel, take the nightly dose, and hope sleep will come to me fast and empty. A few months before I met Kim, I ended up in a psychiatric hospital after not sleeping for a week, the first days because I wanted to finish a painting, the next because I couldn't stop thinking. I knew I was returning to sanity the morning it occurred to me that offering us crazies Cocoa Puffs for breakfast was the overnight nurse's idea of a joke. I should get some Cocoa Puffs, for old time's sake.

Lying beside Kim, I think about how I once calculated a year's supply of Pampers costs twenty-five hundred dollars, and then I consider how none of this matters—Pampers and Cocoa Puffs—

since Cedric's outed me as racist since I was stupid and hassled a middle-aged dude who's trying, just like me, to find a way to get somewhere better than where he's stuck, and maybe I got mad at him because he's just like me, and maybe that proves I'm no racist since self-loathing isn't hatred of the other. I pray, *Dear God, soothe us when we hurt, correct and forgive us when we sin, welcome us into your loving kingdom when we die.* I agree with Kim to have sex while her fellow librarian Mary watches, but then Kim worries Mary will want a three-way, and Kim and I hide in the bathroom of my grandparents' house and do it perched on the edge of the bathtub while peeking out the window at Mary, who sits at a picnic table, elbows on the table and chin in her hands, and then Mary's in my lap, and we're having sex, and Kim's sitting at the picnic table, and I worry I'm not wearing a rubber and Mary will give me a disease and Kim will therefore know I've been unfaithful, and I worry Mary will get pregnant, which will make Brett furious because Mary and Brett are husband and wife, and then I look down and notice Kim's now the one I'm having sex with, and her belly is flat and her crotch shaved, and then the alarm is ringing and Kim's getting out of bed, pregnant beneath one of my T-shirts, crotch covered by a pair of yoga pants.

The erection left over from my dream is depressing, but thankfully, I dreamed of having sex with adults, one of them my wife. I need to pee. Since I haven't signed any paperwork, I haven't officially agreed to stop working for the Middle Eastern Institute, therefore technically I'm not yet laid off, and therefore I don't yet have to tell Kim. I lie in bed waiting to hear the toilet flush, the sign I can take my turn.

Kim's spreading peanut butter on an English muffin when I

come into the kitchen. She pats the newspaper on the counter. "I think that stoner kid from down the street stole the sign. I heard him laughing last night, and now it's gone."

Instead of telling her I put it in the Honda and uncorking my bottle of secrets—alone at the bar, accused of pedophilia, unable to stop thinking about having sex with teenagers, accused of racism—I say, "You're having an affair, aren't you?"

She laughs, then frowns. "Are you being sweet or mean?"

Hazel explodes into the room waving Tooth Fairy money, and the distraction allows me to come around the island and hug Kim. "You're beautiful," I tell her, and it's true, she is, beautiful and kind. It's terrible I'm keeping all these secrets.

"Look where that kind of sweet talk leads," she says, playfully shoving me with her belly. "I need to get going. Big jackets, okay?"

From the kitchen, while I cut crusts from Hazel's turkey sandwich, I hear the Civic start and then Kim and the FOR SALE sign head off. The laptop's open on the counter. The child molester's been replaced by an accident that's causing rush hour mayhem on the north side of the Perimeter. I have to hunt to find the article.

My phone buzzes. A text from Bill in HR: *Bring me your resume today!!!* My heart races, and I have to steady myself by pushing my palms flat against the countertop. Bill will ask Ralph about me. If Ralph knows me well enough to know I'm no bigot—and I'm 99 percent sure he does—he'll read Cedric's message as a weird joke and his endorsement will be glowing. If he doesn't know me well enough, he'll forward Cedric's message to Bill and I'll be out of luck. I have to hope Ralph's recognized my kindness and love for all humanity even though I complain to him about forms and football. And then there's that puddle of pee surely Ralph has seen. Who has done his job, and who hasn't?

I don't have time for a shower. I go to the bathroom and paint my pits with deodorant, find the shirt I ironed Sunday and wore to church, knot my tie while trying to decide if I do in fact look like the molester, and put on my Christmas-and-Easter suit and wingtips. I print out my résumé and put it into my bag, put the box of Barbie shoes in too. In the living room Hazel's watching forbidden *My Little Pony*—no TV before school—and she drops the remote when she tries to turn it off. Batteries skitter across the floor, and Pinkie Pie delivers in falsetto a heartfelt apology for some slight done Applejack.

"Mommy said I could," my child lies. She looks me up and down. "Oh, my," she drawls. "Daddy Fancypants."

"Come here and tell me something." She follows me into the kitchen, and I point to the mug shot I enlarged before I got dressed. "Does he look familiar?" She examines the photo, and I wish I hadn't asked because if she says he looks like me I'm going to cry, but what she says is, "He's sad. Those numbers behind his head mean he's in trouble, right? What did he do?"

"Crashed a truckload of sod into a mail truck," I tell her, mashing up the news. "The numbers show how tall he is," I instruct.

Thankful because someone who's seen my face nearly every day of her life doesn't see any resemblance, I let her fuss over which shoes to wear for much longer than I would usually. Finally she chooses the almost-unworn black-and-pink cowboy boots Zelda's mother gave us because Zelda disliked the shininess of the patent leather. They're cool, but they make me feel poor since I didn't buy them and probably would've balked if

Hazel had seen them in a store and asked: fifty dollars at least. Full-time employment would make me worry less about affording boots, Pampers, Barbies, onesies, chapter books, organic baby food, summer day camps. The sun's out, but it's a cold morning. Maybe a face-to-face apology would make Cedric reconsider his complaint. Hazel is listing aloud the boots' merits as I consider how even imagining begging his forgiveness proves I'm not racist—but maybe I am if the apology is self-serving, even if earnest.

"Is he still up there?" Hazel asks, and I look toward the empty sky. The trees are January bare.

"Is who still up where?"

"Jesus, on the cross."

Thoughts of Sunday school lessons following praise of new boots.

"They took him down," I tell her, "and they put him into a tomb and sealed it with a stone—a big stone."

"I wish it would snow," she says. "You're lucky that where you grew up it snowed. It's not fair."

Above us on the telephone wires, a mockingbird runs through its songbook and then flies to harass a squirrel that's climbed the pole.

"Whoa," Hazel says, "the rarely seen battle between bird and squirrel."

Sometimes, because I spend so little time with other children, I forget how off-kilter is her view of the world, how what she finds funny is unlike what most other six-year-olds find funny. When she says things like "the rarely scene battle," I feel a mix of pride and sadness: She's so smart, but soon she won't need me to teach her anything. I hope she doesn't hate me when the baby's born, and I hope I can both stay loyal to her and love my son.

At the corner Eugenia, who's in Hazel's class, and her mom—Jennifer? Jessica?—are waiting in their matching knit hats, orange with yellow floppy antlers. Eugenia's mom's wearing the necklace she has on every day, and when I greet her, I see the charm I've thought for months was an Arabic letter is instead a tiny gold AK-47. The light changes, we cross, and the girls run ahead, laughing. I'm pleased with myself for never before looking at this woman's chest closely enough to recognize the charm, but I worry there's something more than modesty to my mistaking a machine gun for an Arabic letter—have I conflated a language with violence?

"I'm sorry," she says.

I croak, "What?"

She points to my throat. "Someone died?" She's talking about the tie, the suit—thank God—not the news, not my job, not that she thought I was looking at her neckline.

I make myself laugh, and then I fib, "I've got an interview." I should wear a shirt with a collar more often. In a cheerful voice I say, "I should wear a shirt with a collar more often."

Down the street toward us speeds a Jack Russell. The dog passes the girls, then makes a hard right into the yard we adults are in front of and starts digging under an azalea. The terrier makes a weird strangled noise, and I realize out loud, "Cat." Eugenia's mom says, "Shit," and without thinking, I take three quick paces and drag the dog from under the bush by its stubby tail. It's got a tabby by the back of its neck. I get some fingers under the dog's collar and jerk the Jack Russell up until it's dangling in the air, choking and cycling its legs, but it keeps his jaws locked until I box its ear. It drops the cat, which in a flash is up a tree and hissing at us. When I put the dog down, it wags its tail and seems to be smiling at me, and I fight the urge to kick it.

"That's a bad dog," Eugenia says.

"You stupid jerk!" Hazel yells at it.

"Whose blood is that?" Eugenia's mom asks, and the girls gasp.

It's all over my hands. I've still got the Jack by its collar. When I snap my fingers to make it look up at me, I see the cat's cut its ear. "It's the dog's."

A woman dragging a leash hurries down the sidewalk. "Sorry!" she screams. She's barefoot and wearing sweatpants and a T-shirt even though it's cold enough for ski masks. The Jack Russell barks happily at her. "Thanks," she says when she gets to us and leashes the dog.

I show her my bloody hands. "He got a cat."

"And the cat got him!" Hazel adds.

On cue the tabby hisses from the branch above us. The woman looks up and says, "Oh, no, not Turbo."

"First bell," Eugenia whines. "We're going to miss first bell."

"Why, Elvis?" the woman asks the dog.

"Let's go," Hazel says, and she and Eugenia are off.

We parents follow in silence until we turn the corner and Eugenia's mother whispers, "Why, Elvis?" and we both laugh.

"What?" Hazel wants to know.

"Just talking about the dog," I tell her.

First bell hasn't rung, and a crowd of kids and parents are bottlenecked at the front door. While we wait, Hazel tells everyone who will listen the story of how I saved Turbo. One dad with graying muttonchops slaps me on the back. Another with almost identical sideburns nods. A third, oddly clean-shaven, says, "All right," in an impressed way. I feel foolishly proud to show off my bloody hands. From the diaper bag on the handlebars of her jogging stroller, a mom gives me a baby wipe. The bell sounds, I lean to hug Hazel, and she says, "That was cool," before running off to tell someone else, "My dad saved a cat!" To my kid I'm a hero who saves cats, not a loser or a jerk, and for a moment my worries seem distant, like it was last week, not twenty minutes ago, when I'd been fretting about Cedric and the job in the Art Department and the housepainter at Roebuck's and the child molester in Talbotton.

I head for the train station. In front of me another mom with a double stroller stops when she gets to the co-op chicken coop and from underneath pulls a bag of bread crusts like those I cut off Hazel's sandwich every morning. When I pass, she smiles. The stroller's half-empty, one kid dropped off, a baby snoozing. This is what I want for Kim: feeding crusts to the hens with the baby instead of going to work because I make enough to single-handedly pay the bills.

More moms pushing strollers, many empty, and an old guy walking a huge poodle cross my path by the high school. The sun's rising too slowly. In the shadows I wish I'd worn my big jacket like Kim told me to. Something rattles in my bag when I stick in my hand to get my wallet at the station: the Barbie shoes. I want Hazel to have this many pairs of heels for her dolls. I want the job in the Art Department.

Standing on the platform, I think about the text I could send Ralph—*I didn't yell at Cedric, I just asked him to mop the floor because there was urine on it*—but again I wonder if defending myself makes me look guilty. The train comes, and sitting beside each other in the car I step into are doppelgängers of the housepainter and Cedric, or maybe my mind's a little fogged since riding the subway with me there're also doubles of a bunch of girls I went to high school and college with, all of them in stirrup pants and with hairdos like Pat Benatar. One's wearing a Fishbone T-shirt, for goodness' sake.

Maybe I should rehearse an apology on the guy who with every stop looks less and less like Cedric. The housepainter, however, is the housepainter. He's staring, and I look at my hands, folded in my lap, hoping he can't figure out how he knows me. Between stations he figures it out, stands up, points at me, and screams, "That's the motherfucking motherfucker!"

The Pat Benatars turn, and I recognize a couple of Art undergrads. Sitting beside one of them is a young black woman covering her toddler's ears as he gawks, wide-eyed, at the hollering housepainter. The train slows. I stand and square my shoulders. I'm wearing a jacket and a tie, and he hasn't yet made it home from the bar. My résumé's in my bag.

"There're kids here," I say firmly. "Sit down and shut up."

The train jerks to a stop, and the housepainter falls into his seat, muttering. He doesn't follow me off.

On the platform the women dressed like Emily and Dianne give me high-fives. On the escalator they talk of Basquiat. The sun's up at last, and it's turned January into springtime. I nearly skip along, so buoyant do I feel.

On the way to HR, I detour to the Middle Eastern Institute. I want to see Ralph's face, see if I can tell what he thinks about Cedric's message, but he's not there.

The smell in the hallway is so terrible I can't stop myself from going into the men's room to look. A gray-green border of god-knows-what encircles the puddle of murky piss. I was right to be angry, but my anger was and is worthless. Either I'm totally fucked because I snapped at Cedric and tomorrow I'll have no job anywhere, or Ralph and everyone else will overlook Cedric's complaint and scolding him about the floor will be a dumb thing I got away with because everyone wants to avoid trouble. No one wants strife. Better to use a different men's room, to find a toilet that's not so nasty. Better to swallow disquiet until it keeps you up into the small hours and makes you shit blood.

I told the housepainter to shut up. The text I send Brenda the realtor from the lavatory lets her know her services are no longer needed. After I go to HR, I'll find Kim in the library and admit I was laid off, that I didn't meet Brett at the bar.

From the corner of my eye I can see in the mirror over the dirty sink a reflection of myself as I let down my fly and start adding to the puddle. I back slowly, urinating onto the tiles. Still pissing, I open the door with my free hand. In the hallway I make a new puddle, a bright double of the one below the urinal.

When I look up, Cedric's at the end of the corridor, smirking and shaking his head. We know each other. We work together. We don't want trouble, but we won't run away from trouble if it refuses to leave us alone.

"Karl Marx," he says calmly, "you're batshit."

I shake off, dress left, zip.

Acknowledgments

For your friendship, honesty, and support, thank you Michael Griffith, Nicola Mason, Brian Kiteley, Greg Dobbin, Scott Bocim, Michael Martone, Christopher Merkner, Margaret Luongo, Victor LaValle, Joshua Harmon, David Leavitt, Heather Russel, John Holman, Sheri Joseph, Beth Gylys, Randy Malamud, Jim Crace, Tom Williams, and Patrick Ryan. Thanks also to everyone at Louisiana State University Press, especially James Long, Elizabeth Gratch, Neal Novak, Margaret Lovecraft, and Barbara Neely Bourgoyne.

Many of these stories were first published in *Epoch*. Thank you, Michael Koch, for decades of encouragement and generosity. Others appeared in *Antioch Review, Black Warrior Review, Carolina Quarterly, Cincinnati Review, Colorado Review, Copper Nickel, DIAGRAM, Electric Literature, French Quarter Fiction, New Delta Review, New Flash Fiction Review, New Micro: Exceptionally Short Fiction, New World Writing, Not Normal, Illinois: Peculiar Fictions from the Flyover, One Story, Subtropics, Sundog,*

21st: The Journal of Contemporary Photography, and *Western Humanities Review.*

Thanks Karen Donovan and Walker Rumble at Oat City Press, Carl Annarummo at Greying Ghost Press, and Kelly Dulaney and William Todd Seabrook at The Cupboard Pamphlet for publishing some of the smallest of these stories in the chapbooks *Winter on Fifth Avenue, New York, Pretend You'll Do It Again,* and *Suburban Folktales.*

I'm grateful for the support provided by two Georgia State University Department of English Summer Research Awards.

Thank you, Nin Andrews, for giving me your blessing to quote from "Defining the Orgasm" in "Young Woman Standing before a Window." Photographs from Shana and Robert ParkeHarrison's *Promisedland* inspired "Report Concerning the Occurrences at B——." The italicized quotations in "Moscow" are translations of Vladimir Lenin's writings.

A note regarding "Suburban Folktales": Every night for many, many years I read to my daughter from the two hundred stories collected in *Italian Folktales Selected and Retold by Italo Calvino.* Almost without fail, each evening there was a line or two that struck me, my kid, or both of us as interesting or funny, weird or troubling. In daylight I'd revisit those lines, and if they still made me laugh or cringe (or laugh and cringe), I'd create a suburban folktale by sampling Calvino's versions of stories already many times reimagined: by the storytellers who told and retold them; by Calvino, who collected and edited them; by George Martin, who translated them from Italian to English; and by Calvino again, who edited Martin's translations. My versions of "The Palace of the Doomed Queen," "The Handmade King," "The Ship with Three Decks," "Sleeping Beauty and Her Children," "The Parrot," and "Cannelora" begin with verbatim lines from Calvino's tales of the same titles. "Wooden Maria" opens with a line borrowed from "The Mangy One." "The Sleeping Queen" begins with a fragment from that tale, and the first line of "The Daughter of the Sun" is slightly altered from Martin's translation of Calvino's retelling. Calvino, in his introduction to *Italian Folktales,* writes that he thinks of himself "as a link in the anonymous chain without end by which folktales are handed down, links that are never merely instruments or passive transmitters," and quotes a Tuscan proverb to explain further his method: "The tale is not beautiful if nothing is added to it." I hope that by insinuating myself into the chain I have added a little beauty to these tales.

CPSIA information can be obtained
at www.ICGtesting.com
Printed in the USA
FSHW011252070721
83030FS